There was only one way that Luca would be able to justify claiming Sophia as his own. Only one way he would be able to justify having her in his bed for life.

The child.

That, no one would be able to argue with. And yes, it would come at the cost of an ugly scandal. The things that would be written about them...

They would not be kind.

Those headlines would exist, and it was something that their child would have to contend with. Something they would have to contend with.

But in the end, the memory would fade, and they would be husband and wife longer than they had ever been stepbrother and stepsister.

In the end, it would work.

Because it had to.

He was not in the mood to allow the world to defy him. He was not in the mood to think in terms of limits.

He had for far too long.

He was a king, after all.

And for too long he had allowed that to limit him.

No more.

Maisey Yates is a *New York Times* bestselling author of more than seventy-five romance novels. She has a coffee habit she has no interest in kicking, and a slight Pinterest addiction. She lives with her husband and children in the Pacific Northwest. When Maisey isn't writing, she can be found singing in the grocery store, shopping for shoes online and probably not doing dishes. Check out her website, maiseyyates.com.

Books by Maisey Yates

Harlequin Presents

The Greek's Nine-Month Redemption
Carides's Forgotten Wife

Brides of Innocence

The Spaniard's Untouched Bride
The Spaniard's Stolen Bride

Heirs Before Vows

The Spaniard's Pregnant Bride
The Prince's Pregnant Mistress
The Italian's Pregnant Virgin

Once Upon a Seduction...

The Prince's Captive Virgin
The Prince's Stolen Virgin
The Italian's Pregnant Prisoner

Visit the Author Profile page
at Harlequin.com for more titles.

Maisey Yates

HIS FORBIDDEN PREGNANT PRINCESS

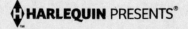

HARLEQUIN PRESENTS®

Recycling programs
for this product may
not exist in your area.

ISBN-13: 978-1-335-53860-4

His Forbidden Pregnant Princess

First North American publication 2019

Printed in U.S.A.

www.Harlequin.com

HIS FORBIDDEN
PREGNANT PRINCESS

To Nicole Helm, ask and you shall receive.
Dare and I shall deliver. Can I make a children's
cartoon a romance novel? Yes. Yes I can.

CHAPTER ONE

SHE WAS BENEATH him in every way. From her common blood to her objectively plain appearance—that years of designer clothing, professional treatments from the finest aestheticians and beauticians and the work of the best makeup artists money could buy had failed to transform into true beauty—from the way she carried herself, to the way she spoke.

The stepsister he had always seen as a particularly drab blot on the otherwise extravagant tapestry of the royal family of San Gennaro.

The stepsister he could hardly bear to share the same airspace with, let alone the same palace.

The stepsister he was now tasked with finding a suitable husband for.

The stepsister he wanted more than his next breath.

She was beneath him in every way. Except for the way he desired most.

And she never would be.

There were a thousand reasons. From the darkness in him, to the common blood in her. But the only reason that truly mattered was that she was his stepsister, and he was a king.

"You requested my presence, Luca?" Sophia asked, looking up at him with a dampened light in her blue eyes that suggested she was suppressing some emotion or other. In all probability a deep dislike for having to deal with him.

But the feeling was mutual. And if he could endure such an indignity then Sophia—in all her borrowed glory—certainly could.

"I did. As you know, it was my father's final wish that you be well cared for, along with your mother. He wrote it into law that you are part of this family and are to be treated as a daughter of his blood would be."

Sophia looked down, her lashes dark on her pale cheek. She had visible freckles that never failed to vex him. Because he wanted to count them. Because sometimes, he wanted to kiss each one.

She should cover them with makeup as most women of her status did. She should have some care for the fact she was a princess.

But she did not.

Today she wore a simple shift that made her bare legs seem far too long and slender. It was an ungainly thing. She also wore nothing at all to cover them. She had on flat shoes, and not a single piece of jewelry. Her dark hair hung limp around her shoulders.

He could only hope she had not gone out in public that way.

"Yes," she said, finally. Then those dark eyes connected with his and he felt it like a lightning bolt straight down to his stomach. He should not. For every reason cataloged in his mind only a moment before. She was not beautiful. Not when compared to the elegant women who had graced his bed before her. Not when compared to nearly any other princess the world over.

But she captivated him. Had done from the moment he had met her. At first it was nothing more than feeling at turns invaded and intrigued by this alien creature that had come into his life. She had been twelve to his seventeen when their parents had married.

Sophia had possessed a public school education, not a single hint of deportment training and no real understanding of the hierarchy of the palace.

She had a tendency to speak out of turn, to

trip over her feet and to treat him in an overly familiar manner.

Her mother was a warm, vivacious woman who had done much to restore his father's life, life that had drained away after the loss of his first wife. She was also a quick study, and did credit to the position of Queen of San Gennaro.

Sophia, on the other hand, seemed to resist her new role, and her new life. She continued to do so now. In little ways. Her bare legs, and her bare face, as an example.

His irritation with her had taken a sharp turn, twisting into something much more disturbing around the time she turned sixteen. That sense of being captivated, in the way one might be by a spider that has invaded one's room, shifted and became much more focused.

And there had been a moment, when he had found her breathless from running out in the garden like a schoolgirl when she had been the advanced age of seventeen, that everything had locked into place. That it had occurred to him that if he could only capture that insolent mouth of hers with his own she would finally yield. And he would no longer feel so desperately beguiled by her.

It had only gotten worse as the years had

progressed. And the idea of kissing her had perverted yet further into doing much, much more.

But it was not to be. Not ever.

As he had just told her, his father had decreed that she was family. As much as if they were blood.

And so he was putting an end to this once and for all.

"He asked me to take care of you in a very specific fashion," Luca continued. "And I feel that now that it has been six months since his passing, it is time for me to see those requests honored."

A crease appeared between her brows. "What request?"

"Specifically? The matter of your marriage, *sorellina*." Little sister. He called her that to remind himself.

"My marriage? Shouldn't we see to the matter of me getting asked to the movies first, Luca?"

"There is no need for such things, obviously. A woman in your position is hardly going to go to the movies. Rather, I have been poring over a list of suitable men who might be able to be brought in for consideration."

"You're choosing my husband?" she asked, her tone incredulous.

"I intend to present you with a manageably sized selection. I am not so arrogant that I would make the final choice for you."

Sophia let out a sharp, inelegant laugh. "Oh, no. You're only so arrogant that you would inform me I'm getting married, and that you have already started taking steps toward planning the wedding. Tell me, Luca, have you picked out my dress, as well?"

Of course he would be involved in approving that selection; if she thought otherwise she was delusional. "Not as yet," he said crisply.

"What happens if I refuse you?"

"You won't," he said, certainty going as deep as his bones.

He was the king now, and she could not refuse him. She would not. He would not allow it.

"Why wouldn't I?"

"You are welcome, of course, to make a mockery of the generosity that my father has shown to your mother and yourself. You are welcome, of course, to cause a rift between the two of us."

She crossed her arms, cocking one hip out to the side. "I could hardly cause a rift between the two of us, Luca. No matter what you might say, you have never behaved as a loving older brother to me."

"Perhaps it is because you have never been a sister to me," he said, his voice hard.

She would not understand what that meant. She would not understand why he had said it.

And indeed, the confusion on her face spoke to that.

"I don't have to do what you tell me to." She shook her head, that dark, glossy hair swirling around her shoulders. "Your father would hardly have forced me into a marriage I didn't want. He loved me. He wanted what was best for me."

"This was what he thought was best," Luca said. "I have documentation saying such. If you need to see it, I will have it sent to your quarters. Quarters that you inhabit, by the way, because my father cared so much for you. Because my father took an exceptional and unheard-of step in this country and treated a child he did not father as his own. He is giving you what he would have given to a daughter. A daughter of his blood. Selecting your husband, ensuring it is a man of impeccable pedigree, is what he would have done for his child. You are welcome to reject it if you wish. But I would think very deeply about what that means."

* * *

Sophia didn't have to think deeply about what it meant. She could feel it. Her heart was pounding so hard she thought she might pass out; small tremors running beneath the surface of her skin. Heat and ice pricking at her cheeks.

Oh, she wasn't thinking of what this meant in the way that Luca had so imperiously demanded she do.

Luca.

Her beautiful, severe stepbrother who was much more king of a nation than he was family to her. Remote. Distant. His perfectly sculpted face only more desperately gorgeous to her now than it had been when she had met him at seventeen. He had been beautiful as a teenager. There was no question. But then, that angular bone structure had been overlaid by much softer skin, his coal-black eyes always formidable, but nothing quite so sharp as crushed obsidian as they were now. That soft skin, the skin of a boy, that was gone. Replaced by a more weathered texture. By rough, black whiskers that seemed ever present no matter how often he shaved his square jaw.

She had never in all of her life met a thing like him. A twelve-year-old girl, plucked up from obscurity, from a life of poverty and set down in this luxurious castle, had been utterly and completely at sea to begin with. And then there was *him*.

Everything in her had wanted to challenge him, to provoke a response from all of that granite strength, even then. Even before she had known why, or known what it meant that she craved his attention in whatever form it might come.

Gradually, it had all become clear.

And clearer still the first time she had gone to a ball and Luca had gone with another woman on his arm. That acrid, acidic curling sensation in her stomach could have only been one thing. Even at fourteen she had known that. Had known that the sweep of fever that had gone over her skin, that weak sensation that made it feel as though she was going to die, was jealousy. Jealousy because she wanted Luca to take her arm, wanted him to hold her close and dance with her.

Wanted to be the one he took back to his rooms and did all sorts of secret things with, things that she had not known about in great detail, but had yearned for all the same. Him. Everything to do with him.

As Luca had said not a moment before, he had never thought of her as a sister. He was never affectionate, never close or caring in a way that went beyond duty.

But she had never thought of him as a brother. She had thought of him in an entirely different fashion.

She *wanted* him.

And he was intent on marrying her off. As though it were nothing.

Not a single thing on earth could have spoken to the ambivalence that he felt toward her any stronger than this did.

He doesn't want you.

Of course he didn't. She wasn't a great beauty; she was well aware of that. She was also absolutely and completely wrong for him in every way.

She didn't excel at this royal existence the way that he did. He wore it just beneath his skin, as tailored and fitted to him as one of his bespoke suits. Born with it, as if his blood truly were a different color than that of the common people. As if he were a different creature entirely from the rest of the mere mortals.

She had done her best to put that royal mantle on, but much like every dress that had ever been made for her since coming to live at the palace, it wasn't quite right. Oh, they could measure it all to fit, but it was clear

that she wasn't made for such things. That
her exceedingly nonwaiflike figure was not
for designer gowns and slinky handmade cre-
ations that would have hung fabulously off
women who were more collar and hip bone
than curves and love handles.

Oh, yes, she was well aware of how little
she fit. And how impossible her feelings for
Luca were.

And yet, they remained.

And knowing that nothing could ever happen with him, knowing it with deep certainty,
had done nothing to excise it from her soul.

Did nothing to blunt the pain of this, of
his words being ground into her chest like
shards of glass.

Not only was he making it clear he didn't
want her, he was also using the memory of
his father—the only man she had ever known
as a father—to entice her to agree.

He was right. King Magnus had given her
everything. Had given her mother a new lease
on life, a real life. Something beyond existence, beyond struggle, which they had been
mired in for all of Sophia's life prior to her
marriage to him.

He had met her when she was nothing more
than a waitress at a royal event in the US,

and had fallen deeply for her in the moment they met.

It was something out of a fairy tale, except there were two children to contend with. A child who had been terrified of being uprooted from her home in America and going to a foreign country to live in a fancy palace. And another child who had always clearly resented the invasion.

She had to give Luca credit for the fact that he seemed to have some measure of affection for her mother. He did not resent her presence in the way he resented Sophia's.

She had often thought that life for Luca would have been perfect if he would have gotten her mother and his father, and she had been left out of the equation entirely.

Well, he was trying to offload her now, so she supposed that was proven to be true enough.

"That isn't fair," she said, when she could finally regain her powers of speech.

Luca's impossibly dark eyes flickered up and met hers, and her stomach—traitorous fool—hollowed out in response. "It isn't fair? Sophia, I have always known that you were ungrateful for the position that you have found yourself in your life, but you have just confirmed it in a rather stunning way. You find it unfair that my father wished to see you cared for? You find it unfair that I wish to do the same?"

"You forget," she said, trying to regain her powers of thought. "I was not born into this life, Luca, I did not know people growing up who expected such things for their lives. I didn't expect such a thing for mine. I spent the first twelve years of my life in poverty. But with the idea that if I worked hard enough I might be able to make whatever I wanted of myself. And then we were sort of swept up in this tidal wave of luxury. And strangely, I have found that though I have every resource at my disposal now, I cannot be what I want in the same way that I imagined I could when I was nothing but a poor child living in the United States."

"That's because you were a delusional child," Luca said, his tone not cruel in any way, but somehow all the more stinging for the calm with which he spoke. "You never had the power to be whatever you wanted back then, Sophia, because no one has that power. There are a certain number of things set out before you that you might accomplish. You certainly might have improved your station. I'm not denying that. But the sky was never the limit, sorely not. Neither is it now. However, your limit is much more comfortable, you will find, than it would have been then."

Her heart clenched tight, because she couldn't deny that what he was saying was true. Bastard. With the maturity of adulthood she could acknowledge that. That she had been naive at the time, and that she was, in fact, being ungrateful to a degree.

Hadn't her position in the palace provided her with the finest education she could have asked for? Hadn't she been given excellent opportunities? Chances to run charitable organizations that she believed in strongly, and that benefited all manner of children from different backgrounds.

No, as a princess, she would never truly have a profession, but with that came the release of pressure of earning money to pay bills.

Of figuring out where the road between what she dreamed of doing, and what would help her survive, met.

But the idea of marrying someone selected by her stepbrother, who no more knew her than liked her, was not a simple thing.

And underneath that, the idea of marrying any man, touching any man, being intimate with any man, who wasn't Luca was an abomination unto her soul.

For it was only him. Luca and those eyes as hard as flint, that mouth that was often curled into a sneer in her direction, those large hands that were much rougher than any king's ever should have been. It was only him who made her want. Who made her ache with the deep well of unsatisfied desire. Only him.

Only ever him.

"I will be holding a ball," Luca said, his tone decisive. "And at that ball will be several men that I have personally curated for you."

"You make them sound like a collection of cheeses."

"Think of them however you like. If you prefer to think them as cheese, that's your own business."

Something burst inside her, some small portion of restraint that she had been only just barely holding on to since she had come into the throne room. "How do you know I like men, Luca? You've never asked."

Luca drew back slightly, a flicker in his dark eyes the only showing that she had surprised him at all.

"If it is not so," he said, his tone remote, "then I suggest you speak now."

"No," she responded, feeling deflated, as her momentary bit of rebellion fell flat on its face. "I'm not opposed to men."

"Well," he said, "one less bit of damage control I have to do."

"That would require damage control?"

"How many gay princesses do you know?" he asked. "The upper echelons of society are ever conservative regardless of what they say. And here in this country it would be quite the scandal, I assure you. It is all fine to pay lip service to such things as equality, but appearances, tradition, are as important as ever."

"And I am already a break with tradition," she pointed out.

"Yes," he said, that tone heavy. "My father's actions in granting you the same rights as I have were unheard of. You are not his by blood, and in royal lines blood is everything. It is the only thing."

"I will go to the ball," she said, because there really was no point arguing with Luca once he had made pronouncements. But whatever happened after that... It would be her decision.

But she was too raw, too shocked, from this entire conversation to continue having a fight with him.

He wanted to marry her off to another man. He wanted her to be someone else's problem.

He felt nothing about doing it.

He did not want her.

He's your stepbrother, and even if he did he couldn't have you. As he just said, tradition is everything.

She squared her shoulders. "When is this blessed event?"

"In a couple weeks' time," he responded.

She blinked. "Oh. I'm not certain my mother will be back from France before then."

"She will be. I have already spoken with her."

That galled her. Like a lance through her chest. Her mother, of course, had no idea how Sophia felt about Luca. She told her mother everything. Everything except for that. Everything except for the completely forbidden lust she felt for her stepbrother. But even so, she couldn't believe that her mother had allowed Luca to have this conversation with her without at least giving her a call to warn her first.

"I told her not to tell you," Luca said as if he was reading her mind.

She sniffed. "Well. That is quite informative."

"Do not be indignant, *sorellina*," Luca said. "It is not becoming of a princess."

"Well, I've certainly never been overly becoming as princesses go," she said stiffly. "Why start now?"

"You had better start. You had better start so that all of this will work accordingly."

He looked her up and down. "We need to get you a new stylist."

"I use the same stylist as my mother," she said defensively.

"It doesn't work for you," he said, his tone cold.

And with a wave of his hand he dismissed her, and she was left somehow obeying him, her feet propelling her out of his royal chamber and into the hall.

She clutched her chest, gasping for breath, pain rolling through her.

The man she loved was going to marry her off to someone else. The man she loved was selecting from a pool of grooms for her to meet in two weeks' time.

The man she loved was her stepbrother. The man she loved was a king.

All of those things made it impossible for her to have him.

But she didn't have any idea how in the world she was supposed to stop wanting him.

CHAPTER TWO

"WHAT IS *THIS*?" The disdain in Sophia's tone when Luca presented her with a thick stack of files the following week was—in his estimation—a bit on the dramatic side.

"It is the list of possible husbands to invite to the upcoming ball. I feel strongly that an excess of five is just being spoiled for choice. Plus, you will not have time to dance with that many people. So I suggest you look it over, and find a way to pare them down."

"This is…" She looked up at him, her dark eyes furious. "These are dossiers of…*men*. Photos and personal profiles…"

"How else would you know if you're compatible?"

"Maybe meeting them and going out for dinner?" Sophia asked.

She crossed her arms, the motion pushing her rather abundant décolletage up over the neckline of the rather simple V-neck top she was wearing.

They really needed to get ahold of that new stylist and quickly. She was, as ever, a temptation to Luca, and to his sense of duty. But soon it would be over. Soon he would have his problematic stepsister married off, and then she would be safely out of his reach.

He could have found a woman to slake his lust on, and over the years he had done just that. After all, whatever was broken in him... Sophia should not have to suffer for it.

But during those time periods he had not been forced to cohabitate with Sophia. Always, when he had spent too much time with her, he had to detox, essentially. Find a slim blonde to remind himself that there were other sorts of women he found hot. Other women he might find desirable.

And then, when it was really bad, he gave up entirely on playing the opposite game and found himself a curvaceous brunette to pour his fantasies into. The end of that road was a morass of self-loathing and recrimination, but on many levels he was happy to end up there. He was comforted by it.

But this... Sharing space with her. As he had done since his father had died. No other woman would do. He couldn't find it in him to feel even a hint of desire for anyone else. And that was unacceptable. As all things to do with Sophia invariably were.

"You are not going on dinner dates," Luca said. "You are a princess. You are part of the royal family. And you are not setting up a Tinder profile in order to find yourself a husband."

"Why not?" she asked, her tone defiant. "Perhaps I want nothing more than to meet a very exciting IT guy who might swipe me right off my feet." He said nothing and she continued to stare at him. "Swipe. Swipe right. It's a dating app thing."

"That isn't funny in the least. As I said, you are part of this family." Perhaps if he repeated it enough, if he drilled it into both of them that they were family, his body would eventually begin to take it on board. "And as such, your standards of marriage must be the same as mine."

"Why aren't you looking for a wife yourself?" she asked.

"I will," Luca said. "In due time. But my father asked that I make your safety, your match, a priority."

He would marry, as duty required. But it would not be because of passion. And certainly not because of love. Duty was what drove him. The preservation of reputation, of the crown. If that crumbled, his whole life was nothing.

He would choose a suitable woman.

Sophia was far from suitable.

"What about the production of an heir?" Sophia lifted a brow. "Isn't that important?"

"Yes. But I am a man, and as such, I do not have the same issues with a biological clock your gender does."

"Right," she huffed. "Because men can continue to produce children up until the end of their days."

"Perhaps not without the aid of a blue pill, but certainly it is possible."

For a moment she only blinked up at him, a faint pink tinge coloring her cheeks. Then Sophia's lip curled. "I find this conversation distasteful."

"You brought up the production of heirs, not me."

She scowled, clearly having to take his point, and not liking it at all. "Well, let me look through the dossiers, then," she said, lifting her nose and peering at him down the slender ridge, perfecting that sort of lofty look that was nothing if not a put-on coming from Sophia.

Though, possibly not when directed at him.

"Erik Nilsson. Swedish nobility?"

"Yes," Luca responded. "He's very wealthy."

"How?"

"Family money, mostly. Though some of it is in sheep."

"His money is in sheep?" Sophia asked, her expression completely bland. "Well, that is interesting. And one would never want for sweaters."

"Indeed not," he said, a vicious turn of jealousy savaging his gut. Which was sadistic at best. To be jealous of a man whose fortune was tied up in sheep and who had the dubious honor of being a minor noble in some small village that wasn't part of the current century.

A man he had not expected his stepsister to show the slightest interest in. And yet, here she was.

"So he will have access to...wool. And such," Sophia said. "And...he's quite handsome. If you like tall and blond."

"Do you?" he asked.

"Very much," she said with a strange injection of conviction. "He's on the table." She set the folder aside. "Let us get on with the next candidate, shall we?"

"Here you are," he said, lifting up the next folder and holding it out toward her. "Ilya Kuznetsov."

She arched a brow. "Russian?"

He raised one in response. "Very."

Sophia wrinkled her nose. "Is his fortune in vodka and caviar?"

"I hate to disappoint you but it's in tech. So, quite close to that IT guy you were professing to have a burning desire for."

"I didn't say I had a burning desire for anyone," she pointed out, her delicate fingers tracing the edge of the file.

He couldn't help but imagine those same fingers stroking him.

If he believed in curses, he would believe he was under one.

"I don't know anything about computers," she continued, setting the folder off to the opposite side of the first one. "I prefer sheep."

She was infuriating. And baffling. "Not something you hear every day. Now, to the next one."

She set aside the next two. An Italian business mogul and a Greek tycoon. Neither one meeting up to some strange specification that she blathered on about in vague terms. Then she rejected an Argentine polo player, who was also nobility of some kind, on the basis of the fact that a quick Google search revealed him to be an inveterate womanizer.

"You're not much better," she said mournfully, looking up from her phone.

"Then it is a good thing that I am not in the files for consideration."

Something quite like shock flashed through her eyes, and her mouth dropped open. Color flooded her cheeks, irritation, anger.

"As if that would ever happen. As if I would *consider* you." She sniffed very loudly.

"As my sister, you could not," he bit out.

"Stepsister," she said, looking up at him from beneath her dark lashes.

His gut twisted, his body hardening for a moment before he gathered his control. The moment seemed to last an eternity. Stolen, removed from time. Nothing but those eyes boring holes through him, as though she could see right into him. As though she could see his every debauched thought.

Every dark, terrible thing in him.

But no, there was no way she could.

Or she would run and hide like a frightened mouse.

"In terms of legality, in terms of my father's will, you're my sister," he said. "Now, the next one."

She went through the folders until she had selected five, though she maintained that the Swedish candidate was top of her list.

It did not escape his notice that she had selected all men with lighter features. Diametrically opposed to his own rather dark appearance.

He should rejoice in that.

He found he did not.

"Then these are the invitations that will be sent out," he said. "And I will be reserving dances with each of the gentlemen."

"Dances?" She blinked. "Are we in a Regency romance novel? Am I going to have a card to keep track?"

"Don't be ridiculous. You can keep track of it in an app."

She barked out a laugh. "This is ridiculous. You're ridiculous."

"Perhaps," he said, "but if you can think of a better way to bring together the most eligible men in the world, I'm all ears."

"And what happens if I don't like any of them?"

"You're very excited about the sweaters."

"What if I don't like any of them?" she reiterated.

"I imagine something will work out."

"I'm serious," she said, her blue eyes blazing with emotion. "I'm not marrying a man I don't like because you have some strange time frame you need to fulfill."

"Then we will keep looking."

"No," she said. "I promise that I will be fair, and I will give this a chance. But if it doesn't work, give me six months to make my own choice. If I can't find somebody that is suitable to me, and suitable to you, then I will let you choose."

"That was not part of the original bargain."

Six months more of her might just kill him.

"I don't care," Sophia said. "This isn't the Dark Ages, and you can't make me do what I don't want to. And you know it."

"Then you have a bargain. But you will have to put in serious effort. I am not wasting my time and resources."

"Well I'm not marrying a man just to suit you, Luca. I want to care for the man I marry. I want to like him, if I can't love him. I want to be able to talk to him. I want him to make me laugh."

Luca braced himself. Braced himself for her to start talking about passion. About wanting a man who would set her body on fire.

She didn't.

She had stopped at a man who made her laugh, and had not said she wanted a man who would make her come. He shouldn't think such thoughts. Shouldn't want to find out why that didn't seem to occur to her.

Why attraction didn't come into her lists of demands to be met.

It made him want to teach her. Didn't she understand? That physical desire *mattered*?

And if she didn't understand…

Some Swedish sheep farmer would be the one to teach her.

Luca gritted his teeth. "But do you need to want him, *sorellina*?"

He should not have asked the question. He shouldn't entertain these thoughts, and he certainly shouldn't give voice to them.

Cursed.

If he weren't a logical man, he would swear it.

"Want him?" she asked, tilting her head to the side.

"Yes," he bit out. "Want him. His hands on your body. His mouth on yours. Does it matter to you whether or not you want him inside you?"

He hadn't realized it, but he'd moved closer to her with each sentence. And now he was so near her he could smell her. That delicate, citrus scent that always rose above the more cloying floral or vanilla perfumes the women around the palace typically favored. A scent

he was always assured he could pick out, regardless of who else was around. Always Sophia, rising above the rest.

"I... I..." Her cheeks blushed crimson, and
then she stood, her nose colliding with his
cheek before she wobbled backward. "I've
only ever wanted one man like that." The
words seemed to be stuck in her throat. "I
never will again. I'm sure. And I refuse to
discuss it. Least of all with you."

And then she turned and ran from the
room.

CHAPTER THREE

SINCE MAKING A fool out of herself in front of Luca days earlier, Sophia had done her best to avoid him. It wasn't that difficult. Luca was always busy with affairs of state, and it was actually for the best. The problem was that every time she heard heavy, authoritative footsteps on the marble floors of the palace, her heart caught, and held its position as if it was waiting, waiting to bow down to its king.

She did not want Luca to be the king of her heart. Being King of San Gennaro was quite enough power for one man. But her heart didn't listen. It beat for Luca, it stopped for Luca, tripped over itself for Luca.

It was starting to feel like she was running an obstacle course every time she made any movement in the palace. One wherein Luca was the obstacle that she was trying desperately to avoid.

But she wanted to see him, too. That was the real conundrum. The fact that she wanted to both avoid him and be with him all the time. Foolish, because he wasn't even nice to her. He never had been. But still, he captivated her in ways that went beyond sanity.

And today there would be no more avoiding him as he had engaged the services of a new stylist to help her prepare for the ball. The ball wherein she was supposed to choose a husband.

Luca and those dossiers had enraged her. She had picked every man who was completely opposite to him, to spite herself, mostly.

She highly doubted that she would marry any of these men. But one thing she knew for certain was that she would not marry a man who was simply a pale carbon copy of her stepbrother. She would not choose a man who was tall, dark and handsome, who had that kind of authority about him that Luca possessed. Because it would simply be an effort at giving her body a consolation prize. And that was far too tragic, even for her.

She shouldn't be tragic, she mused as she wandered down the labyrinthine hall toward the salon where she was meeting the new stylist. She had been a commoner, and she had been raised up to become the princess of a country. She had been adopted by a king. A man who had loved her, and had loved her mother. Who had shown them both the kind of life that neither of them had ever dreamed possible.

But Luca. Always Luca.

It was as though her heart was intent on not being happy. As though it wanted to be tragic. In the same way that it had determined that Luca would be its owner.

In a palace, a life of luxury, and with that came a fervent, painful love for the one man she could never have.

And, he didn't like her.

Star-crossed lovers they were not. Because Luca could hardly stand to share the same space as she did. He thought she was silly, that much was apparent from their exchange yesterday. They were from completely different worlds. The man couldn't understand why she found it off-putting to be looking through file folders filled with profiles of men she had never met, trying to work out which one of them she could see herself marrying.

Although she supposed it wasn't entirely different from online dating.

No. She refused to pretend that any of this was reasonable. It wasn't.

She wondered if she would ever find someone who just wanted *her*. These men, who had agreed to come to the palace, would never have done so if she wasn't a princess.

It was the only reason her biological father had ever spoken to her. After he'd seen her mother in the media, marrying King Magnus.

King Magnus had loved her. But…he had only strived to love her because of her mother.

And Luca…

Well, nothing seemed to make Luca like her at all. Not status, or herself.

He was consistent, at least.

She took a deep breath, bracing herself for the sight of him. That was another problem with Luca. Too much exposure to him and her poor heart couldn't recover between moments. Not enough, and it always flung itself against her breastbone as though it were trying to escape. Trying to go to him. To be with him.

Her heart was foolish. And the rest of her body was worse.

She gathered herself up, drew in the deepest breath possible, hoping that the burning in her lungs would offset the rest of her physical response. That it might drown out the erratic tripping of her pulse.

Then, she pushed the door open.

And all the breath left her body in a rush.

There was no preparing for him. No matter how familiar she was with his face, with that imposing, muscular physique of his, it was like a shock to her system every time. Those dark eyes, eyes that she sometimes thought might see straight through her, but they couldn't. Because if they did, then he would know. He would know that she was not indifferent to him. He would know that her feelings toward him were in no way familial.

He would be disgusted by her.

It took her a while to notice that there was a woman standing next to him. The new stylist, presumably. It took her a while, because as far as she was concerned when Luca was in the room it was difficult to tell if anyone else was there at all.

"You must be Princess Sophia," the woman said. "I'm Elizabeth."

"Nice to meet you." Belatedly, she decided that she should try and curtsy or something, so she grabbed the edge of her sundress and bent forward slightly. She looked up and saw that Luca was watching her with a disapproving expression on his handsome face.

If she bowed down and called him King of the Universe he would disapprove. He was impossible.

"She needs something suitable for an upcoming event," Luca said. "She must look the best she ever has."

"I am confident that I can accomplish such. It is simply a matter of knowing what sort of energy Sophia should be projecting. All these colors that she's wearing now are far too drab. And from what I have seen in pictures and publications over the years, her overall color palette doesn't suit her. I have plans."

Suddenly, Sophia felt very much like she was being stared down by a hungry spider. And she was a fly caught in the web.

"Just leave it to me," she said, shooing at Luca.

"I must approve the selection," he said. Obviously not taking kindly at all to being shown the door in his own palace.

"You will approve," Elizabeth said, her tone stubborn. "You will see soon."

The rest of the afternoon was spent styling and plucking and scrubbing.

Sophia felt as though she had been exfoliated over every part of her body. This woman did not try to have her hair completely straightened, but rather, styled it into soft waves, which seemed to frame her face better, and also—so she said—would not revert halfway over the course of the evening.

Which was the problem that Sophia usually had with her hairstyles. Her hair wasn't curly, but it was not board-straight, either, and it could not hold such a severe style for hours on end. It became unruly when she got all sweaty. And she supposed it was not a good thing to sweat when you were a princess, but she did.

Then there was the matter of the gown she chose. None of the navy blue, black or mossy-green colors that her mother's stylist favored. No, this gown was a brilliant fuchsia, strapless with a sweetheart neckline that did nothing at all to cover her breasts. It draped down from there, skimming her waist, her full hips. Rather than making her look large like some of the high-necked gowns that had been chosen for her before, or blocky like the ones that hit her in strange places at the waist, she actually looked…curvy and feminine.

Typically, she didn't show this much skin, but she had to admit it was much more flattering when you could see that she had cleavage, rather than a misshapen mono breast.

Her lipstick matched the dress, and her eye makeup was simple, just black winged liner. Her cheeks were a very bright pink, much brighter than she would have normally done, but all of it created a very sophisticated effect. And for the first time she thought maybe she looked like she belonged. Like maybe she was a princess. Not a girl being shoved into a mold she resolutely could not fit into, but one who'd had a mold created just for her.

"He will approve of this," Elizabeth said.

"You know he is my stepbrother," Sophia pointed out. "He doesn't need to approve of it in that way."

The very idea made her face hot. And that she wanted him to…that she wanted him to want her was the worst humiliation of all.

"I know," the woman said, giving her a look that was far too incisive. "But you wouldn't mind if he did."

Sophia sputtered. "I… He can't."

"That has nothing to do with what you feel. Or what you want."

Sophia felt like she had been opened up and examined. Like her skin had been peeled away, revealing her deepest and most desperate secrets. She hated it. But she didn't have time to marinate in it because suddenly, the door was opening, and Luca had returned. Obviously, Elizabeth had texted him to say that Sophia was ready. But she wasn't ready. She wasn't ready to face him, not with the woman next to her knowing full well how Sophia felt about Luca. Because now she felt like it was written across her skin, across her forehead, so that it could clearly be read by the man himself.

Her earlier confidence melted away, and her skin began to heat as Luca stopped, his dark eyes assessing her slowly.

Her body tingled, her breasts feeling heavy, her nipples going tight as though his fingertips were grazing her skin. As if he was doing more than simply looking.

"It will do," he said, his tone as hard as his features.

Her throat felt prickly, and she swallowed hard, feeling foolish, her heart fluttering like a caged bird trying to escape. How could she feel so much when he looked at her, while he felt nothing for her at all? While he clearly saw her as an annoyance.

He didn't look impressed; he didn't look awed or surprised with what she had felt was a total transformation.

"I am glad that I reach at least the bottom of your very lofty standards, Your Majesty," she said stiffly. "I can only hope that a certain Swedish noble has a slightly more enthusiastic response."

"I said that it will do," he reiterated. "And it will. What more do you want from me, *sorellina*?"

"I spent the entire day receiving a make-over. I would have thought it would garner a response. But it seems as if I am destined to remain little more than wallpaper. It is okay. Some women are never going to be beautiful."

She grasped the flowing skirt of her dress with her fists and pushed past Luca, running out of the room, down the hall, running until her lungs burned. The sound of the heels she was wearing on the floor drowned out the sound of anything else, so it wasn't until she stopped that she heard heavy foot-steps behind her. And she was unprepared for the large, strong hand that wrapped around her arm and spun her in the oppo-site direction. It was then she found herself gazing up into Luca's impossibly dark and imposing eyes.

"What is it you want from me?" he asked, his voice low and hard. Shot through with an intensity she had never heard in his voice before. "What do you want me to give you? What reaction would have been sufficient? In the absence of the one man you have ever wanted, what is it you expected *me* to give you? Do you want me to tell you that you're beautiful? Do you want me to tell you the curves would drive any man to distraction?

That every man in that ballroom is going to imagine himself holding you in his arms? Feeling those luscious breasts pressed against his chest? Kissing those lips. Driving himself inside you? Is that what you want to hear? I can give you those words, Sophia, but they are pointless. I could tell you that any man who doesn't want you was a fool, but what is the point in saying those words? What could they possibly mean between the two of us?" He released his hold on her, and she stumbled backward. "Nothing. They mean nothing coming from me. It will always be nothing. It must be."

"Luca…"

"Do not speak to me." He straightened then, his expression going blank, his posture rigid. "It will do, Sophia. You will wear that dress the night of the ball. And you will find yourself a husband. I will see to that."

It wasn't until Luca turned and walked away, wasn't until he was out of her sight, that she dropped to her knees, her entire body shaking, her brain unwilling to try and figure out what had just passed between them. What those words had meant.

He said it could be nothing. It was nothing. She curled her fingers into fists, her nails digging into her skin.

It was nothing. It always would be.

She repeated those words to herself over and over again, and forced herself not to cry.

CHAPTER FOUR

HE HAD ACTED a fool the day that Sophia had received her makeover. He had… He had allowed his facade to crack. He had allowed her to reach beneath that rock wall that he had erected between himself and anyone who might get too close.

He never acted a fool. And he resented the fact that Sophia possessed the power to make him do so.

His entire life was about the crown. The country.

His mother had driven the importance of those things home before she died. In an exacting and painful manner. One that had made it clear it was not Luca who mattered, but San Gennaro. The royal name over the royal himself.

He had shaped himself around that concept.

But Sophia had looked…

Thankfully, it was time. The guests had all arrived for the ball, with Sophia scheduled to arrive fashionably late so as to draw as much attention as possible.

His attention had been fixed on her far too much in the past few days. Sadly, everything his body had suspected about her beauty had been confirmed with this recent makeover. This stylist had managed to uncover and harness the feminine power that had always been there. And she had put it on brilliant display. Those curves, not covered anymore, but flaunted, served up as if they were a rare delicacy that he wanted very much to consume.

And of course, other men were going to look at her this way. Other men were going to dance with her.

Another man was going to marry her. Take her to his bed.

It was the plan. It was his salvation. Resenting it now… Well, he was worse than a dog in the manger, so to speak. Much worse.

He made a fox and a hen house look tame. Of course, if he were the fox he would devour her. He would have no one and nothing to answer to.

He was not a fox. He was a king.

And he could not touch her. He *would* not.

He would honor that final request his father had made. To keep her safe. To see her married to a suitable man.

He was not that man, and he never could be.

Even if their relationship wasn't as it was, he would not be for her. He might have been, once. But that possibility had been destroyed along with so many other things. He had very nearly been destroyed, too. But as he had set about to rebuild himself, he had made choices. Choices that would redeem the sins in the past. Not his sins to redeem. But that mattered little.

He was the one who had to live with the consequences. He was the one who had to rule a country with strength and unfailing wisdom.

And so, he had purposed he would.

But that did not make him the man for her.

Thank God the ball was happening now. Thank God this interminable nightmare was almost over.

She would choose one of the men in attendance tonight. He would be certain of that.

He stood at the back of the room, surveying the crowd of people. All of the women dressed in glorious ball gowns, none of whom would be able to hold a candle to Sophia, he knew. None of whom would be able to provide him with the distraction that he needed.

"This is quite lovely." He turned to see his stepmother standing beside him. She had been traveling abroad with friends for months, clearly needing time away to process the loss of her husband. Though she was back now, living in a small house on palace grounds.

It suited her, she said, to live close, but no longer in the palace.

She had lost a significant amount of weight since the death of his father, and she had not had much to lose on that petite frame of hers to begin with. She was elegant as ever, but there was a sadness about her.

She had truly loved his father. It was something that Luca had never doubted. Never had he imagined she was a commoner simply looking to better her station by marrying royalty. No, there had been real, sincere love in their marriage.

Something that Luca himself would never be able to obtain.

"Thank you," he said.

"And all of this is for Sophia?"

"Yes," he said. "It is as my father wished.

He wanted to see her in a good marriage. And I have arranged to see that it is so."

"Yes," she said, nodding slowly. "But what does Sophia think?"

"She has agreed. In that, she has agreed to try to find someone tonight. And if she does not, she has six months following to choose the man that she wishes. But I have confidence that one of the men tonight will attract her."

"I see," she said.

"You do not approve?"

"I married your father because I loved him. And one of the wonderful things that came with that marriage was money. With money came the kind of freedom that I never could have hoped Sophia to have if we had remained impoverished. I hate to see it curtailed."

"This is not curtailing her freedom. It is simply keeping with what is expected of those in our station. I have explained this to Sophia already."

"Yes, Luca. I have no doubt you have. You are very like your father in that you are confident that your way is always correct."

"My way is the best for a woman in her position. You must trust that I am the authority on this."

"You forget," his stepmother said, "I have been queen for a sizable amount of time. I did not just leave the village. So to speak."

"Perhaps not. But I was born into this. And you must understand that it is difficult to marry so far above your station. That is not an insult. But I know that it took a great deal for yourself and Sophia to adjust to the change. I know that Sophia still finds it difficult. Can you imagine if she married someone for whom this was foreign?"

"You make a very good point."

"This ball, this marriage, is not for my own amusement." It was for his salvation. However, he would leave that part unspoken.

Suddenly, the double doors to the ballroom opened, and all eyes turned to the entryway. There she was, a brilliant flash of fuchsia, her dark hair tumbling around her shoulders. She was even more beautiful than he had remembered. Golden curves on brilliant display, her skin gleaming in the light.

"Oh, my," her mother said.

"She got a new stylist," he said stiffly.

"Apparently."

Sophia descended the staircase slowly, and the moment one foot hit the bottom of the stair, her first suitor had already approached her. The Swede.

Sophia would probably be disappointed he didn't have a sheep on a leash to entertain her. Or a sweater.

"You do not approve of him?" his step-mother asked.

"Of course I approve of him. I approve of every man that I asked to come and be considered as a potential husband for Sophia."

"Then you might want to look less like you wish to dismember him."

"I am protective of her," he said, straightening and curling his hands into fists.

"If you say so."

He gritted his teeth. He did not like the idea that his stepmother of all people would find him transparent. He prided himself on his control, but Sophia tested it at every turn.

And so he told himself that the feeling roaring through him now was relief when the man took hold of Sophia and swept her around the dance floor.

The other man's hand rested perilously low on her waist, on the curve of her hip, and if he was to move his hand down and around her back he would be cupping that lovely ass of hers. And that, Luca found unacceptable.

He will not stop there if he marries her. He will touch her everywhere. Taste her everywhere. She will belong to him.

He gritted his teeth. That was the point. The point was that she needed to belong to another man, so that he could no longer harbor any fantasies of her.

As the song ended, another man approached Sophia, and she began to dance with him. Another of her selections.

Luca approached a woman wearing royal blue, and asked her to dance. Kept himself busy, tried to focus on the feel of her soft, feminine curves beneath his hands. Because what did it matter if it was this woman, or another. What did it matter. Sex was sex. A woman's body was a woman's body. He should be able to find enjoyment in it. He should not long for the woman in pink across the room. The woman who was tacitly forbidden to him. But he did.

The woman he held in his arms now might well have been a cardboard cutout for all that she affected him.

But still, he continued to dance with her, knowing that he should not. Knowing that dancing with any single woman this long would create gossip. He didn't even know her name. He wouldn't ask for it. And tomorrow he would not remember her face until he saw it printed in the paper. She didn't matter.

Suddenly, Sophia extricated herself from

her dance partner's hold, excusing herself with a broad gesture as she scurried across the ballroom.

"Excuse me," he said, releasing hold of his dance partner, following after his stepsister.

Sophia wove through the crowd and made her way outside. He followed. But by the time he got out to the balcony, she was gone. He looked over the edge and saw a dark shape moving across the grass below. He could only barely make her out, the glow from the ballroom lights casting just enough gold onto the ground to highlight her moving shape. He swung his leg over the edge of the balcony and lowered himself down to the grass below, following the path that Sophia had no doubt taken.

He said nothing, his movements silent as he went after her. To what end, he didn't know. But then, he had no idea what she thought she was doing, either. It was foolish for her to leave the ball. And it was foolish for him to go after her. All of this was foolish. Everything with her. Always.

And yet, he couldn't escape her. That was the essential problem. She was unsuitable because of their connection. She was inescapable because of their connection. And for that reason, he had never been able to master it.

He could not have her; neither could he banish her from his life.

And here he was, chasing after her in a suit.

He was the king of a nation, stumbling in the dark after a woman.

Finally, she stopped, her pale shoulders shaking, highlighted by the light of the moon. He reached out, placing his hand on her bare skin. She jumped, turning to face him, her eyes glistening in the light. "Luca."

And suddenly, he knew exactly why he had gone after her. He knew exactly what the end-game was. Exactly why he was here.

"Sophia."

And then he wrapped her in his arms and finally did the one thing he had expressly forbidden himself from doing. He claimed her lips with his own.

CHAPTER FIVE

LUCA WAS KISSING HER. It was impossible. Utterly and completely impossible that this was happening. She was delusional. Dreaming. She had to be.

Luca *hated* her.

Luca saw himself as being so far above her that he would hardly deign to speak to her if they weren't related by marriage.

He didn't want to kiss her. He didn't.

Except, with the little bit of brainpower that she had, she recalled that moment in the halls of the castle days ago. When she had gotten her makeover. He had grabbed hold of her arm and had told her he could not tell her how beautiful she was because it was pointless. Because nothing could come of it.

Did that mean he wished it could?

It had all felt like something too bright and too close then. Something she couldn't parse and didn't want to. Not when the end result would only be her own humiliation. Even if he didn't know what she was thinking, entertaining the notion that Luca might want her had always seemed horrific, even if no one ever found out.

It was so surreal a thought that she was still asking it even as those firm, powerful lips thrust hers apart, his tongue invading her mouth.

She had never been kissed like this before. Had never received anything beyond polite kisses that had seemed to be a testing of her interest.

Luca, true to form, was not testing her interest. He was *assuming* it. And she imagined that if he found her disinterested, he would work with all that he had to change her mind.

Except, his assumption was correct. And she did not possess the strength to deny that. Not now.

Not when her most cherished fantasy was coming to life, right here in the darkened garden of the palace.

Luca cupped her face, large, hot hands holding her steady as he angled his face and took her deeper.

He kissed exactly like what he was. An autocratic conqueror. A man who had never been denied a single thing in his life.

A man who would not be denied now.

"I cannot watch this," he rasped. "I cannot watch other men dance with you. Put their hands on you."

"You said… You said you had to find me a husband." Her voice was wobbly, tremulous, and she hated that. She wished—very much—that she could be more confident. That she could sound sophisticated. As if this was simply another garden tryst of many in a long line of them. Rather than the first time she had truly, honestly been kissed by a man.

Rather than a girl on the receiving end of something she had desired all of her life.

She didn't want him to know that. She didn't want him to know how she felt.

But then she imagined that she betrayed herself with each breath, with each moment that passed when she didn't slap his face and call him ten kinds of scoundrel for daring to touch her in that way.

Of course she betrayed herself. Because, though he had been the one to instigate, she had kissed him back.

She had been powerless to do anything else. She had been far too caught up in it, consumed by it. By him.

The story of her life.

Things went well, and then Luca. And it all went to hell. It all belonged to him.

"I am going to find you a husband," he said. "I swore it to my father." He dragged his thumb along the edge of her lip. "But I cannot pretend I don't want you. Not any longer."

"You... You want me?"

"It is like a disease," he ground out. "To want my *sister* as I do."

"I'm not your sister," she said, her lips numb. "We don't have the same parents. We don't share blood at all."

"But don't you see? To my father you were. And you would be to the nation. An affair between the two of us would have disastrous consequences."

She closed her eyes, swallowing hard. "How?"

"Think of the headlines. About how our parents were married, and I debauched you likely from the moment you were beneath my roof. As a child. Or, you seduced me to try and hold on to your place. The nation has accepted you as a princess, without a blood relation, but reminding them so starkly that you do not carry royal blood is only a mistake. Can you imagine? An affair between two people who must thereafter remain family? It would be a disaster," he reiterated.

"Then why did you kiss me?"

"Because I no longer possess the power to *not* kiss you. He had his hands on you," he growled, grabbing hold of her hips and drawing her up against his body. "You may have only ever wanted one man before me. But I will make you forget him."

She gasped. She could feel the aggressive jut of his arousal against her stomach, could feel the intensity in the way he held her. His blunt fingertips dug into her skin, and she was certain that he would leave bruises behind. But she didn't care. She would be happy to bear bruises from Luca's touch. Whatever that said about her.

And then, he stopped talking. Then, that infuriating, arrogant mouth was back on hers, kissing, sucking and tasting. He angled his head, dragging his teeth along her tender lower lip before nipping her, growling as he consumed her yet again.

Sophia didn't know this game. She didn't know what to do next. Didn't know how to use her lips and tongue just so as Luca seemed to do.

So she battled against inexperience with enthusiasm, clinging to the front of his jacket with one hand, the other wrapped around his tie as she raised herself up on her toes and kissed him with all the needs she had inside her. She found herself being propelled backward, deeper into the garden. There was a stone bench there, and Luca gripped her hips, sliding his large, warm hands down her thighs, holding on to her hard as he lifted her so that her legs were wrapped around his waist. Then he brought both of them down onto the stone bench, with her sitting on his lap.

Her thighs were spread wide, the quivering, needy heart of her pressed hard against that telltale ridge that shouted loudly to her that this wasn't a hallucination. That Luca did want her. That no matter it didn't make any sense, that no matter it went against everything she had always believed about him, about herself, about who they were, it was happening.

He moved his hands back to cup her rear, drawing her even more firmly against his arousal. Heat streaked through her veins, lightning shooting through her body. She had never felt anything like this. Like the all-consuming intensity of Luca. That sure and certain mouth tasting her, the friction slick and undeniably intoxicating. Like those big, hot hands all over her curves. His length between her thighs. He was everywhere. All around her. Flooding her senses. It wasn't just his touch. It was his flavor. His scent.

Familiar and so unfamiliar all at the same time. She knew Luca. From a distance. He had been in her life for so many years. Part of so many formative feelings that she'd had. He had most definitely been her very first fantasy. But those fantasies had been muted. They had not come close to the reality of the man himself. Of what it meant to be held by him, kissed by him, consumed by him.

This was no gauzy fantasy. This was something else entirely. It was harsh, and it was far too sharp. She was afraid it was going to slice her in two. The feelings of pleasure that she felt were nothing like the fluttery sensations that had built low in her stomach when he used to look at her across a crowded room. Were nothing compared to the swooping feeling she would get in her stomach when she would allow herself to imagine something half as racy as him kissing her on the mouth.

No. This was pain. Sharp between her legs. A hollow sensation at her core that terrified her, because she didn't feel as though he had created it just now so much as uncovered it. That she was hollow until she could be filled by him. That if he didn't, she would always remain this way.

Luca.

This was a raw, savage uncovering of desire. Desire that she had always known was there, but that had been muted, blunted, by her innocence. By the sure certainty that nothing could ever happen between them.

But now he wanted her. And she didn't know if she was strong enough to bear it.

Because it wasn't just what might happen next. No. It was what would happen when it ended. Then it would end. He had said as much.

He might have confessed his desire for her, but there were no other feelings involved. He had spoken of nothing tender. No. It was nothing but anger in Luca's eyes. Anger and lust.

That was what had been on his face when he had chased her down in the corridor days ago. Anger. Rage. And lust. The unidentified emotion in his eyes. The one she had not been brave enough to identify.

He moved his hand up the back of her head, cupping her skull, then he plunged his fingers deep into her locks, curling his hand into a fist and tugging hard, forcing her head backward, pressing his lips to the curve of her throat. And she felt like wounded prey at the mercy of a predator. Her most vulnerable parts exposed to him.

And yet she allowed it. Didn't fight against it. Wanted it.

Needed it.

That was the worst part. This was something more than want. This was part of her essential makeup.

She had been exposed to Luca at such an early age that he had been formative to her. That he was part of her journey to womanhood. So maybe this was apt. Terrifying though it might be, maybe this was something that needed to happen.

This wasn't the Middle Ages. None of those men out in the ballroom had been promised a virgin princess.

She owed them nothing, for now. For now, it was only Luca.

For now.

And that would have to be enough.

"Dear God," he rasped, dragging his tongue along the edge of her collarbone, down lower to where the plump curve of her breasts met the neckline of her dress. "I've lost my mind."

"I…" She was going to say something witty. Something about the fact that she had lost hers right along with him. But she couldn't speak. Instead, she heaved in a sharp breath, bringing that wicked mouth into deeper contact with her breast. He growled, jerking the top of her dress down, exposing her to him.

She had never been naked in front of a man before. She found she wasn't embarrassed. Certainly, the darkness out in the garden helped, but she knew that with the aid of the moonlight he could still see plenty. But it was Luca. The only man that she had ever been prepared to have seen her naked body. The only man she had ever fantasized about. This was terrifying. It went far beyond anything she had imagined. But it was with him.

And that made all the difference. It made every difference.

He said some words in Italian that she didn't understand. She was fluent enough, having lived in San Gennaro for so much of her life, but she didn't know these words. Hot and filthy-sounding, even without the translation. He scraped his cheek along that tender skin, his whiskers abrading her skin. And then he drew one aching, tightened nipple deep into his mouth, sucking hard.

She arched her back, crying out as pleasure pierced her core like an arrow.

He brought one hand up to cup her breast, rough and hot. She wanted to ask him why his hands were so rough. Wanted to ask him what he did to keep his body so finely honed. Why a man who should have the body of any man with a desk job looked as he did.

But she couldn't ask. All of her words, all of her questions, were bottled up in her throat, and the only thing that could escape was one hoarse cry as he moved from one breast to the next with his mouth, sucking the other nipple in deep, teasing her and tormenting her as he did.

For a moment she had the thought that this was too much too soon. She wasn't ready for this. How could she be? She had never even kissed a man before, and now she was in the arms of King Luca, her top pulled down, her breasts exposed. Riding the hard ridge of his arousal. How could that not be too much? How could she possibly withstand such a thing?

But suddenly, perhaps in time with the flex of his hips upward—that iron part of him making contact with the place where she was softest, most pliant and most sensitive— perhaps it was that that crystallized everything for her. It wasn't enough. And she had waited a lifetime for it. It didn't matter what experience or lack of it she'd had before. Not in the least. What mattered was that it was him.

That she had longed for, craved, desired this very thing for what felt like an eternity.

Luca. Her stepbrother. The man who seemed for all the world to find her utterly and completely beneath his notice, was kissing her. And she could not deny him anything that he wanted.

She could not deny herself what she wanted.

Luca's large, warm hands slid down the shape of her body as if he was taking her measurements with those strong fingers. Then they moved down farther, to her thighs, finding the hem of her dress, already pushed up partway, and shoving it up farther, exposing her even more.

He made a low, feral sound. Hungry. Untamed. Perhaps he was like this with all women; that was a possibility. One that she didn't want to think about. At least not too much. She would like to be special. But she had no idea how she could be. Anything between them was impossible, and she knew it. She had always known it. That didn't mean her feelings disappeared.

"I have wanted you," he said, his voice rough, as rough as the scrape of his whiskers against the side of her neck as he dragged a kiss down her throat. "It is a madness. It is like a sickness. And nothing…nothing has ever come close to banishing it from me. You are like a poison in my blood."

The words sounded tortured. Tormented. And for a moment she wondered if he felt even the slightest bit of what she had felt over the past years. And if he did… Then whatever this could be, and she had no illusions that it could be anything remotely close to permanent, she knew it was the right thing.

Madness. Sickness. Poison.

Those words described what she felt for Luca far too closely. They resonated inside her. They were her truth. And if they were his…how could she deny it?

She was no longer content to simply sit on his lap and be kissed. No. She wanted him. She wanted this. And she was going to have him.

She returned volley with a growl of her own, biting his lower lip as she moved her hands to that black tie that held his crisp, white shirt shut. With trembling fingers she undid the knot and pulled it open, then made quick work of the top button of that shirt. Followed by the next. And the next. She pushed the fabric apart, exposing muscles, chest hair and hot, delicious skin to her touch.

She had heard people talk about desire. But they had never said that it was so close to feeling ill. So close to feeling like you might die if you couldn't have what you wanted.

So close to pain.

There was a hollow ache between her legs, running through her entire body, and she felt that if it was not filled by him she wouldn't be able to go on. It was as simple as that.

She traced her fingertips over his chest, across his nipple, gratified by the rough sound of pleasure that exited his mouth as she did so. He wrapped his arms around her tightly, lowering his head again, tasting and teasing her breasts as he did. She had never imagined that insanity could be blissful. But hers certainly was. Magical in a way that she had not imagined it could be. She had not thought that there could be beauty in torment. But there was. In this moment.

In this world they had created in the rose garden, separate from the concerns happening in the ballroom. The concerns of their lives, real lives, and not this stolen moment.

There were men in there that she was expected to consider seriously as husbands. A whole raft of duties and responsibilities waiting for both of them that had nothing to do with satisfying their pleasure under a starry sky with only the moon as witness.

But she was glad they had found this.

This quiet space. The space where only they belonged. Where their parents' marriage didn't matter. Where their titles didn't matter. Where—whatever that could possibly mean to a man like Luca—they simply were Luca and Sophia, with nothing else to concern them.

He kept on saying things. Rough. Broken. Words in Italian and English. Some of which she couldn't understand, not so much because of the language barrier but because of the intensity in his words, the depth of them. The kinds of things he said, talking about doing things she had never imagined, much less spoken about.

But they washed over her in a wave, and she found she wanted them all. That she wanted this.

Him.

Broken, and out of control in a way that she had never imagined it was possible for Luca to be. At all other moments he was the picture of control. Of absolute and total certainty. And in this moment he did not seem as though he had the power to be that man.

It made her feel powerful. Desired.

His hands moved between her thighs, sliding between the waistband of her panties and teasing her where she was wet and ready for him. For a moment she felt a fleeting sense of embarrassment, a scalding heat in her cheeks. Because certainly now he would know how much she wanted him. How much she felt for him. What woman would be like this if she didn't? And there, he found the incontrovertible evidence. But if it bothered him, he didn't show it. Instead, he seemed inflamed by it. Seemed to want her all the more.

"Perhaps later," he rasped, kissing her neck, her cheek, making his way back to her lips. "Perhaps later I will take my time. Will be able to savor you as you should be. But now… I find there is not enough time, and I must have you."

She wanted him to have her. Whatever that might mean. She needed it.

He shifted, undid the closure on his pants and wrapped his arms tightly around her, angling her hips so that she was seated above him, the head of his arousal pressing against the entrance to her body.

And then he thrust up into her, deep and savage, giving no quarter to her innocence at all. It hurt. But Luca didn't seem to notice. Instead, he began to move inside her in hard, decisive thrusts. She couldn't catch her breath. But then, she didn't want to. Even as she felt like she was being invaded, conquered, she didn't want him to stop. Even as it hurt, she didn't want him to stop. Gradually, the pain gave way to pleasure, an overwhelming, gripping sense of it that built inside her until she thought she wouldn't be able to take it much longer.

When it broke over her it was like a wave containing a revelation, pleasure like she had never known bursting through her. If she had looked up to find fireworks in the sky she wouldn't have been surprised. But the only thing above her was stars. The fireworks were in her.

They were the fireworks.

She and Luca together.

She held on to him tightly as she rode out her release, pulsing waves that seemed to go on and on crashing inside her endlessly. Then he gripped her hips hard, driving himself up into her with brute force as he found his own release, a growl vibrating through his chest as he did.

And then somehow, it was over. Nothing but the sound of their breathing, the feel of his heart pounding heavily against her hand, where it rested against his sweat-slicked chest.

The night sky no longer seemed endless. Instead, it pressed down on them, the reality of what had just occurred lowering the blackness but leaving the stars out of reach.

She felt dark. Cold.

She was cold. Because she was naked in a garden.

Luca moved her away from him, beginning to straighten his clothing. "We must go back," he said, his tone remote and stiff.

"How?" she asked. Because she had a feeling he did not just mean to the ball, but to the way things had been before he had touched her. Before that rock wall had broken between them and revealed what they had both desired for so long.

"It doesn't matter how. Only that it must be."

She looked at him, searching his face in the darkness. "I don't know if I can."

"But you must," he said, uncompromising.

The light from the moon cast hollows of his face into light and shadow, making it look as though he was carved out of the very granite his voice seemed to be made of.

"You will go back into that ballroom and you will dance with the rest of the men you said you would dance with. Then you will choose a husband," he continued.

"Luca," she said, her voice breaking. "I can't do that. Not after I was just…"

"It is only sex, *sorellina*," he said, the endearment landing with a particular sharpness just now. "You will find a way to cope."

Panic attacked her, its sharp, grasping claws digging into her. "I was a virgin, you idiot."

That stopped him. He drew back as though he had been slapped.

"You said…you said you wanted a man."

She looked away, her shame complete now, her face so hot she was sure she was about to burst into flame. "Who do you think I wanted, you fool?"

The silence that fell between them was heavy. As if the velvet sky had fallen over the top of them.

"Not the choice I would have made my first time. But the choice was yours. You had every chance to say no. You did not." Suddenly his tone turned fierce. "Am I to assume you didn't want to? Are you trying to imply that you didn't know what you were doing?"

"No," she said. "I knew what I was doing."

"Then I fail to see what your virginity has to do with any of it. This is hardly Medieval times. No one will expect a virgin princess on their wedding night anyway."

"I suppose not."

"I must go back. I am the host, after all. Take all the time you need to gather yourself."

He said that as though she should be impressed with his softness. With his kindness. She was about to tell him how ludicrous that was, but then he turned and walked away, leaving her there, half-naked on a stone bench, having just lost her virginity to her stepbrother. To her king.

Her lungs were going to cave in on themselves. Collapse completely, along with her heart. It was shattered anyway, so it didn't matter where the pieces landed.

This was her fantasy. That bright little spot of hope that had existed somewhere inside her, a glimmer of what could be that kept her warm on the darkest of nights.

Now it was gone. Snuffed out. As dark as the night around her.

When she went to bed at night, she would no longer wonder. Because she knew. It had been better than she had imagined. Had transformed her. In more ways than the physical. He had been inside her. Joined to her. This man that had held her emotions captive for half of her life.

This man she'd spent nights weaving beautiful, gilded stories about in her head before she fell asleep. If only. If maybe. If someday.

But it had happened. And now there was no more rest in *if only*.

Nothing remained but shattered dreams.

He acted as though they would be able to go back to normal. But Sophia knew she would never be the same again.

CHAPTER SIX

SOPHIA HAD AVOIDED him for the past few weeks. Ever since she had gone back into the ballroom and proceeded to dance with every man he had commanded her to.

She had been pale-faced and angry-looking, but gradually, it had all settled into something serene, though no less upset.

But he did not approach her. Not again. And she moved around the palace as if she were a ghost.

He had failed her. Had failed them both. But there was nothing to be done. There was no use engaging in a postmortem. His control had failed him at the worst possible moment.

He had done the one thing he had purposed he would never do. And it had been all much more a spectacular failure than he had initially imagined it would be.

A *virgin*.

He had not thought she would be that.

She had gone to university. Had moved out in the world for quite some time, and she was beautiful. In his mind, irresistible. Hell, in practice she was irresistible. Had he been able to resist her, then he surely would have.

No man could possibly resist her. If his own ironclad control had failed…

So perhaps that was his pride. Because clearly she had somehow remained untouched all this time.

And he had failed at maintaining that particular status quo.

But that other man had been touching her. Holding her in his arms.

Perversely, he was satisfied by the fact that he had been the first man to touch her. It was wrong. And he should feel a deep sense of regret over it. Part of him did. But another part of him gloried in it.

As with all things Sophia, there was no consensus between desire and morality.

The only contact he'd had with Sophia had been for her to tell him that she wanted to speak with him today. And so he sat in his office, his hands curled into fists, resting on the top of his desk while he waited for her to appear.

The fact that she never failed to put him on edge irked him even now.

There'd never been a more pointless and futile attraction in the history of the world. Or, perhaps there had been, but it had not bedeviled him, and so, it didn't concern him now. No, it was Sophia who had that power over him.

And she was not for him.

There was no way he could reconfigure their fates to make it so. No way that he could switch around their circumstances. Even if she weren't his stepsister...

He was not the man for her.

The door to his office cracked slightly, and she slipped inside, not knocking. Not waiting for an announcement. Because of course she wouldn't. Of course she would break with protocol, even now. Not allowing the blessed formality inherent in royal life to put some distance between them when it was much needed.

"You wished to come and speak to me?"

"Yes," she said. "But I should think that was self-evident. Considering that I made an arrangement to come and speak to you, and now I am here doing it."

"There is no need to be sarcastic, Sophia."

"I'm surprised you recognized it, Luca."

For a moment their eyes caught and held, the sensation of that connection sending a zap of electricity down through his body.

She looked away as though she had felt that same sensation. As though it had burned.

"I recognize it easily enough. What did you wish to speak to me about?"

"I wanted to tell you that I've made my selection. I've decided who I will marry."

That was the last thing he had expected, and her words hit him with the force of a punch squared to the chest. So intense, so hard, he thought it might have stopped his heart from beating altogether.

"You have?"

"Yes. I hope that you value an alliance with Sweden."

He had not been aware that he possessed the ability to feel finer emotions. Until he felt a last remaining piece of himself—one he had not realized existed—turn to stone. "I'm surprised to hear you say that."

"That I selected him specifically? Or that I have selected anyone at all?"

"That you have complied at all. Rather than making this incredibly difficult."

She clasped her hands in front of her, her dark hair falling down into her face. The outfit she was wearing was much more suited to her than her usual fare. Tight, as that ball gown on the night he had first kissed her had been. A tangerine-colored top that shaped exquisitely to her curves, and a skirt with a white and blue pattern.

But the pattern was secondary to the fact that it hugged her body like a second skin. As he wished he could hug her even now. What he wouldn't give to span that glorious waist again, to slide his palms down to those generous hips.

Having her once had done nothing to eradicate the sickness inside him.

But this marriage… Perhaps it would accomplish what he had hoped it would.

And in the end, he would still have been the one to have her first.

Yes. But he will have her second, if he hasn't had her already, and you will have to watch the two of them together.

He had always known that would be his fate. There was no fighting against it.

"I had some very important questions answered the night of the ball," she said, making bold eye contact with him. "I have no reason to fight against this marriage. Not now."

There was an unspoken entreaty in those words, and it was one he could not answer.

He would have to marry, yes, that was certain. But it would never be a woman like her. It would be a woman who understood. One who didn't look at him with hope in her eyes.

One who wouldn't mind that the part of him that could care for another person, the part of him that loved, had been excised with a scalpel long ago.

That he was a man who ruled with his head because he knew a heart was no compass at all. Least of all his.

It felt nothing. Nothing at all.

"Excellent," he said. "I'm glad there's no longer a barrier."

Color flew to her cheeks, and he did nothing to correct her assumption that he had made an intentional double entendre. He had not. But if it made her angry, all the better.

"Let me know how soon you wish for the wedding to be, and I will arrange it."

"In a month," she said quickly. "We are to be married in a month."

"Then I will prepare an announcement."

Sophia's head hurt. Her heart hurt. Everything hurt. The depression that she had fallen under since the ball was pronounced. It made everything she did feel heavy. Weighted down.

The engagement to Erik hadn't helped matters. The courtship in general hadn't helped at all. And she felt like a terrible person. He was solicitous, kind. Their interactions had not been physical at all. The idea of letting him touch her so closely to when she and Luca had…

Though part of her wondered if she should. Like ripping off a Band-Aid.

The mystery was gone from sex anyway.

A tear slid down her cheek and she blinked, shocked, because she hadn't realized she had been so close to crying. She wiped it away and swallowed hard, attempting to gather herself.

She was currently getting a wedding gown fitted. That meant she had to look a little bit less morose. Though, right now, she was sitting in the room alone, wearing nothing but a crinoline.

Both the seamstress and her mother would be in the room soon, and she really needed to find a way to look as if she was engaged in the process.

But then, she felt as if she had not been engaged in the process of her life for the past few weeks, so why should this be any different?

It had been foolish, perhaps, to jump into marrying Erik, simply because she wanted to do something to strike back at Luca. Simply because she wanted there to be something in her life that wasn't that deep, yawning ache to be with him.

They couldn't be together. It was that simple. He didn't want to be with her. Oh, he had certainly revealed that he lusted after her in that moment in the garden, but it wasn't the same as what she felt for him.

And furthermore, he was allowing her to marry another man.

Another tear splashed onto her hand.

Was that why she was doing this? Was that why she was going through with the engagement? Because she wanted him to stop it?

That was so wholly childish and ridiculous.

And yet she had a feeling she might be just that ridiculous and childish.

The door to the dressing room opened, and the designer and her mother breezed inside at the same time. Her mother was holding the dress, contained in a plastic zip-up bag, and the designer was carrying a kit.

"Let's help you get this on," the woman said briskly.

Sophia's mother unzipped the bag and helped Sophia pull the dress over her head as the designer instructed. There was much pinning and fussing and exclamation, and Sophia tried very hard to match those sounds.

"Are you okay?" her mother asked as the designer was down on her hands and knees pinning the hem of the gown.

"I'm...overwhelmed." She figured she

would go for some form of honesty. It was better than pretending everything was fine when it clearly wasn't, and her mom wasn't going to accept that as an answer.

"It is understandable. This wedding has come together very quickly."

"It's what Luca wants."

"I see."

"It's what Father wanted."

"And what do you want, Sophia? Because as much as I loved your stepfather, and as much as I know he had your best interests at heart… I didn't marry him because I wanted to be queen. I didn't marry him for money, or status. I married him because I loved him. And I want nothing less for you. I understand that he did this because it is what he would have done for his biological daughter if he'd had one. You are not from this world. And you don't have to comply to the dictates of it if you don't wish to."

What was the alternative? Living life with Luca glowering down at her. Wanting him. Watching him get married and have children…

Well, it was that or cutting herself off from her family altogether.

For a moment she stood adrift in that fantasy. Blowing in a breeze where she was tied to nothing and no one. It made her feel empty, hollow. Terrified.

But at least it didn't hurt.

"I want this," she said, resolute. "It's the right thing. And he's a very nice man."

Her mother sighed heavily. "I'm sure that he is."

"You know that Luca wouldn't allow this if he wasn't suitable. If he wasn't good."

"Certainly not," she said. "I know Luca would never allow any harm to come to you. Not physical harm, anyway."

Sophia gritted her teeth, wondering, not for the first time, if her mother suspected that there was something between Luca and herself. If she did, she was not saying anything. Resolutely so.

And Sophia certainly wasn't going to say anything.

She looked down and kicked the heavy skirt of her dress out of the way, and then she straightened, looking at herself in the mirror. Suddenly, she felt dizzy, wobbling slightly as she took in the sight of herself wearing a wedding gown. A wedding gown.

She felt ill.

"Excuse me," she said, clamoring down from the stepstool and dashing into the adjoining bathroom, slamming the door behind her as she collapsed onto her knees and cast up her accounts into the toilet.

She braced herself, shaking and sweating, breathing hard. She had never been sick like that. So abruptly.

She felt terrible. Throwing up hadn't helped.

She pushed herself up, afraid that she had damaged the gown, but it looked intact.

There was a heavy, sharp knock on the door. "Sophia?" It was her mother. Worried, obviously.

"I'm fine," she said. "Just a little bit... nauseated."

"Can I come in?"

"Okay."

The door opened and her mother slipped inside, her expression full of concern. "Are you ill?"

"I wasn't," Sophia said.

"You just suddenly started to feel sick?"

"Yes."

"Sophia..." Her mother looked at her speculatively, "forgive me if this is intrusive... Is it possible that you... Are you pregnant?"

The tentative grasp that Sophia had on the ground beneath her gave way. And she found herself crumbling to the floor again.

"Sophia?"

"I..."

"Are you pregnant?" her mother asked.

"It's possible," she said.

"I suppose the good thing is that the wedding is soon," she said, bending down and grabbing hold of Sophia's chin, her matching dark gaze searching Sophia's. "Are you happy?"

"I'm scared," Sophia said.

She couldn't organize her thoughts. She was late. It was true. She hadn't given it much thought because she had been stressed out with planning the wedding. But she was quite late. And she and Luca had not used a condom that night.

One time.

She'd had sex one time.

With the last man on earth she should have ever been with, and she had gotten pregnant. What were the odds of that happening?

Of course, now she was engaged to another man, a man whose baby it couldn't possibly be, because she had never even kissed him.

But there was going to be a wedding. Invitations had been sent out. Announcements had been made. She was being fitted for a dress.

"Of course you are," her mother said. "It's a terrifying thing facing a change like this. But wonderful." She put her hand on Sophia's face. "You're the best thing that ever happened to me, Sophia."

Sophia tried to smile. "I hope I'll be even half as good a mother as you have been to me."

"You will be."

"I wish I had such confidence."

"You will have help from your husband," her mother said. "I didn't have any help. It will be so nice for you to start with more in life than we had."

Sophia's mouth felt dry as chalk. How could she tell her mother that it wasn't her fiancé's baby?

That it was Luca's.

She couldn't. So she didn't. Instead, she let her mother talk excitedly about the wedding, about being a grandmother. Instead, she went outside and finished the fitting.

When it was over, she walked down the empty halls of the palace, back in her simple shift dress she had been wearing earlier. Then she pushed the door to her bedroom open. She looked around. At this beautiful spectacular bedroom that it was still difficult to believe belonged to her.

She stumbled over to her bed, a glorious, canopied creation with frothy netting and an excess of pillows.

Then she lay across that bed and she wept.
She wept like her heart was breaking.

Because it was.

And she had no idea what to do about it.

CHAPTER SEVEN

ULTIMATELY, SOPHIA FELT it was wisest to procure a test through the official palace physician. The princess was hardly going to go to a drugstore to acquire a pregnancy test. It would be foolish. Things like that could never stay secret, not for long. Not in a media-hungry society, always looking for scandal.

One of the many things she'd had to learn, because it wasn't ingrained. That anyone would be interested in the life and times of a girl like her. But they were now. Because of who her mother had married.

Because of who she was, all thanks to a piece of paper. Nothing more.

Oftentimes, she appreciated what had come from that marriage.

This was one of the times she appreciated it less.

Fortunately, she trusted the woman that she had seen for years, recommended to her by palace staff. And she knew that her confidentiality was in fact one of the most important parts of her role as the physician to all members of the royal family, and palace staff.

Unfortunately, no matter how good the doctor was, she could not change the test results with skill.

Sophia paced back and forth while she waited. She knew pregnancy tests didn't take *that* long. Still, the doctor was certainly taking her time in the makeshift lab, AKA, Sophia's en-suite bathroom.

When the door finally did open, the doctor looked blank. Sophia couldn't read a plus or negative sign on the woman's face. "The test is positive," she said. "Congratulations."

Sophia didn't want to be congratulated. Why should she be? She'd made a massive mistake and put everything Luca believed in in jeopardy. She was risking public embarrassment, wasted money on a wedding… she…she deserved something. But it wasn't congratulations.

"Thank you," Sophia said, instead of any of the things she was thinking. "The wedding is soon at least, so all will be sorted."

Except, she had no idea how to sort it out. This wedding was happening. All of the moving parts were at critical mass.

Tomorrow. The wedding was tomorrow. People were coming from all over to attend.

She was going to have to go to him. She was going to have to see Erik and let him know exactly what transpired. Likely, he would want to break it off. But it was entirely possible that…

She had no idea what she was supposed to do. Was she going to hide Luca's child from him? And what would he think? There was no way he would believe that she had immediately gone to bed with another man. He would know the child was his.

Would he?

It was entirely possible she could convince him she had played the role of harlot. That she had gone straight from Luca, on a garden bench, to Erik's bed.

But Erik was blond, while Luca was dark, darker than she was. The child would not look like Erik.

"I just need some time alone," Sophia said finally. "That's all I need."

The doctor nodded, collecting things and leaving Sophia in her bedroom. Leading her to solve a problem that might well be utterly and completely unsolvable.

She walked over to the closet and opened it

up, letting her hands drift over the silk fabric of the wedding gown that was hanging there.

She was carrying Luca's baby. And she was supposed to walk toward another man tomorrow and say vows to him. Promise to love him, stay with him forever. She was supposed to have her wedding night with him.

A violent wave of nausea rolled over her.

She had been lying to herself this entire time. Thinking that she could do this. Thinking that she could be with another man. That she could make all of her feelings for Luca go away if she only tried hard enough. That if she replaced him in her bed she could replace him in her heart, but she didn't know how that could possibly be.

She swallowed hard, her throat dry. There was no going back. Not now.

There couldn't be. There was so much riding on this. Luca was right. Deals had already been made with Erik regarding his holdings, based on this marriage. Luca's reputation... in the eyes of the people, of the world, it mattered.

San Gennaro's reputation depended on Luca's. And...this could potentially compromise that.

And she had to think of that.

It had nothing to do with her being afraid.

With her feeling raw and wounded. Nothing at all. It was the greater good. Not…not the fact that thinking of Luca hurt.

Yes, Erik she was going to have to talk to. Because she owed her future husband honesty if nothing else.

Luca…

She had a feeling it would not be a kindness to give him honesty.

Her head throbbed, her entire body feeling wrung out. She knew that her logic was fallible at best. She knew that she was wrong in so many ways, but she couldn't untangle it all to figure it out.

She picked up the phone, and she dialed the number she needed to call most.

"Hello?"

"Erik," she said, not sure if she was relieved or terrified that he'd answered. "There's something I need to tell you."

"You are not running out on the wedding, are you?"

"*You* might. When you hear what I have to say." She swallowed. "I'm pregnant."

There was nothing but silence for a moment.

"Well," he said, his tone grim. "We both know it isn't mine."

"Yes. We do. But…no one else has to know

that. It would be for the best if the baby's father didn't know. And I can't have anyone… I can't have anyone knowing." She tightened her hold on her phone, her heart hammering so hard she could scarcely hear herself speak. "But only if that… If it doesn't offend you in some way."

"I cannot say I'm pleased about it. Though I appreciate the fact that you did not try to pass it off as mine."

"I wouldn't have done that," she said quickly. "Before we get married, you have to know the truth."

"Whose is it?" he asked.

She hesitated. "I cannot give you *that* truth. That's the one thing I can't tell. Trust me on this one thing. I know I made a mistake, but I told you this much. I'm not trying to trick you."

"I see," he said, his tone brave. "You didn't know you were pregnant before now?"

"I swear I didn't."

There was a long pause, silence settling over her, over the room, the furniture groaning beneath its weight.

"It is too late to turn back," he said at last. "I require this union with your country. The alliance and the agreements that were promised to me… I want to see them honored. And if we were to cancel the wedding at such a late date the resulting scandal would be a serious issue."

"Yes," she replied, her lips numb. "That is my feeling on it, as well."

"Then we will go ahead with the wedding."

She must have agreed, but she couldn't remember what she said the moment after she'd spoken the words.

Sophia hung up the phone, not feeling any sense of relief at all. She curled up into a ball on the bed as hopelessness washed through her. Tomorrow it would be finished. It would finally be over.

Except, it never would be. Because whatever the world believed, whatever anyone knew...

The child in her womb was Luca's. A part of him. A part of her. The evidence of their passion, of her love. A bright and shining thing that she would never be able to ignore.

But Luca had been clear. There can be no scandal. She would not subject their child to that. She would not subject him to it.

And so she would have to subject herself to this.

For the second night in a row, Sophia cried herself to sleep.

* * *

The morning of the wedding dawned bright and clear, and Sophia awoke feeling damaged. Empty.

Except she wasn't empty. She was carrying Luca's child.

That fact kept rolling through her mind on a reel all while her hair was fixed, her makeup done, her gown given its final fittings.

Her mother looked at her with shining eyes, pride in them. Misplaced.

So badly misplaced.

"Are you all right?" she asked.

"Nervous," she said honestly.

It echoed the exchange they'd had during the fitting. But it was all the more real now. Her tongue tasted like metal, her whole body like a leaden weight.

"Did you take a test?" her mother asked.

"Yes," Sophia said.

"And?"

"It's positive," Sophia returned. "I'm having a baby."

Her mother held her for a long time before letting her go finally. "Have you told Erik?"

"Yes."

If her mother thought something was amiss—and Sophia thought she might—the other woman said nothing. Instead, they continued readying themselves for the ceremony. Then, a half hour before everything was set to begin, Sophia was ushered into a private room where no one could see her. Where the big reveal of the bride would be preserved.

It was dark in there. Quiet. The first moment of reflection she'd had all day. Her veil added an extra layer of insulation against reality. And gave her too much time to think.

She resented it. She didn't want to reflect on anything. She wanted all of this to be over.

She wanted it done, so that there was no going back. She wanted her wedding night done.

Wanted that moment to pass so that Luca would no longer be the only one who'd had claim on her body. So that perhaps she could start building some sort of bond with Erik.

As if you believe that will work.

She had to. What other choice did she have? Tell her *stepbrother* she was having his baby? A stepbrother who didn't seem to want her as more than a physical diversion? Even if it wasn't for the potential scandal...

Luca had been more than willing to send her straight to the arms of another man out of his sense of duty, after taking her virginity in an open space where anyone could have caught them.

Yes, on some deep level she felt this was a betrayal of Luca, but she felt as if he had betrayed her first.

He had made no move to stop this wedding. None at all. He was truly going to let her marry another man.

Then she realized that all this time she had been hoping he would stop it. That he would step in. He said he could not stand to have another man touch her, as he had done the night of the ball.

In the end she had hoped, beyond reason, beyond anything, that he would make this stop.

But he had not.

The realization was like a hot iron through her chest. What a fool she was. She'd been clinging to hope, even now. Hope was why she was here. Because she kept imagining…

She squeezed her eyes shut, a tear streaming down her cheek.

She would be damned if she would go crawling to him. Confess to him she was pregnant with his child when he had already made it clear he did not want her.

And perhaps it was wrong. Perhaps she had no right to those feelings.

Perhaps, as the father, regardless of the fallout, he should be made aware of the baby.

But she couldn't.

Because what if he stopped it all then? What if that was the only reason?

How could she live with herself after that? How could she live with him?

Suddenly, the door to her little sanctuary burst open. His hands clenched into fists, his expression unreadable.

Luca.

CHAPTER EIGHT

Rage rolled through Luca like a thunderstorm. There she was. His duplicitous stepsister. Her expression obscured by a veil, her figure a stunning tease in that virginal-looking gown.

They both knew she wasn't a virgin.

He had been the one to ruin that, to ruin her. He was well aware.

And then there was the other bit of evidence that she was not as innocent as she currently appeared to be.

"Are you here to give me away?" she asked, her tone maddeningly calm.

"Is that what you want? You want me to march you out of here and pass you off from my arm to his? Fair enough, as you seem to have gone from my bed and straight into his."

He waited for her to correct him on that. But she did not.

"It's a bit late to be acting possessive, *fratello*."

The word *brother* stabbed into him. Sharp. Enraging. The reason she was here prepared to marry another man in the first place.

"Is it now?" It did not feel too late. It felt altogether like just the right time.

She took a step back, stammering. Wondering if she had overplayed her hand. "I'm in a wedding gown. The guests have all arrived. I assume there is a priest."

"You know as well as I do that there is."

"Then unless you intend to give me to my groom, symbolically, of course, I suggest you step aside."

He crossed his arms, standing between Sophia and the door. "Absolutely not."

"I need to go, Luca," she said, her tone pleading with him.

"Answer me one question first," he said, taking a step toward her. His heart was pushing the limits of what a man could endure, he was certain, his stomach twisted.

"What question?" she asked.

"Have you slept with him?" He asked the question through gritted teeth, his entire body tense.

She turned to the side, the veil a cascade of white and bland separation, concealing her expression from him. "I don't see how that's any concern of yours."

"It is my concern if I say it is," Luca returned. "Answer the question, Sophia. And if you lie to me, I will find out."

Suddenly, her posture changed. She came alive. As though she'd been shocked with a live wire.

"Oh, no," she said, delicate hands balled into fists. "I haven't slept with him. But I intend to do so tonight. I would show you the lingerie I selected, but that would be a bit embarrassing. After all, you are only my very concerned stepbrother."

A red haze lowered itself over Luca's vision.

Anger was like a living thing inside him, roaring, tearing him to pieces. He had no idea what answer he would have preferred. One that proved she had been touched by another man, but might not be attempting to deceive them both...or this.

She was doing exactly what he had suspected. And by admitting that, she had also confirmed what he had suspected, his heart raging, when those lab results had come across his desk only an hour ago.

He had imagined...

He had imagined that she would come to him if the news was relevant to him.

She had not. But there was a chance. He had known that. Even if she had slept with Erik the day after she had been with him, there would be a chance.

And here, she had made it very clear, that there was only one possibility.

Still, she hadn't come to him. As if on some level she knew. Knew she should not bind herself to him. As if she could see the cracks in his soul.

If he were a good man, if any of his outward demonstrations of royal piety were deeper than skin, he would let her be.

Would let her go off and marry Erik.

But he had reached an end. An end to the show he had lived for the past two decades.

An end to anything remotely resembling *good*.

"We will have to send our regards to Erik," he said, taking a step forward.

"Why is that?"

"Because I…" He reached forward, grabbing the end of her veil, lifting it and drawing it over her head, revealing that impossibly lovely face that had called to him for years now. That was his constant torment. His constant desire. "I am about to kiss his bride for him."

Luca drew her into his arms; she was his

now. There was no denying it. There was no other alternative.

When they parted, she was staring at him, wide eyed.

"And he," Luca continued, his voice rough, "is about to find himself without a wife."

Then he lifted her up and threw her over his shoulder, ignoring the indignant squeak that exited her lips.

"What are you doing?" She pounded a fist against his back.

They were turning into a bad farce of a classic film. And he didn't care. Not one bit.

"Well," he said, continuing to hold her fast. "It seems that we have skipped a few steps. Here you are, in a wedding dress, but our relationship has already been consummated. And it appears that you are pregnant with my child."

"Luca!"

"Did you think I wouldn't find out?" He carried her out of the chapel and across the lawn. It was private back here; paparazzi and guests both barred from coming into this section of the grounds, where the bride might be disturbed. And here, Luca had a private plane waiting.

Just in case.

Just in case of this exact moment.

It felt like madness. Like something that had overcome him in the moment. Strong enough he'd had to pick her up and haul her off.

But obviously some of his madness was premeditated.

Though he had not envisioned this exact scenario, it was clear to him now there had never been another possible outcome.

"Forgive me," he said, not meaning at all. "But I feel as though at this moment in time a wedding ceremony is a bit redundant. We are headed off on our honeymoon."

"We can't," she protested, beating against him again with one closed, impotent fist.

A rather limp, ineffective protest, all in all. When the poor creature could scarcely move.

"I am the king, *sorellina*. And I can do whatever I want."

Yes. He was king. And he could do whatever the hell he wanted. He had been far too caught up in being honorable. In being dutiful to his country. In doing as his father had asked. In doing as his country expected.

In protecting Sophia. Making sure she had the life that would best suit her, not the one that would best please him.

What the hell was the point of being king if you didn't take everything that you desired?

And he desired his stepsister. She was also carrying his heir.

That meant that she would be his.

Regardless of what anyone thought.

It was all clear and bright now. As if the sun had come out from behind the clouds.

"What if I refuse?" she asked.

He carried her up the steps, onto the plane, holding her still while his staff secured the cabin. None of them daring to question him. "You're not in a position to refuse," he said as he placed her in one of the leather seats and solicitously fastened her seat belt. "You are only in a position to obey."

She didn't speak to him for the entirety of the flight. He supposed on some level that was understandable.

She simply sat there and looked at him, radiating rage and tulle, resembling an indignant cake topper. Disheveled, from his carrying her out across the lawn and onto the plane, her hot eyes bright and angry, that lovely lace wedding gown making her look the perfect picture of a bride.

She would need a new wedding gown for when they married. As beautiful as she looked now he would be damned if she walked down the aisle toward him in a dress she had meant for someone else.

That was not something he could endure. He found that he was quickly getting to the end of his endurance where she was concerned.

Scandal was something to be avoided at all costs. It was something his mother had drilled into his head even after she had known…

She had protected the reputation of the family.

And now he was about to destroy that. Then it called into question a great many things.

But here was the point where he had to break from his desire to prevent scandal.

Because if there was one thing, one bitter shard of anger that existed in his chest that cut deeper than all the others, it was the fact that his mother had prized reputation over protecting her son.

Over pursuing retribution for him.

She had cared more for her marriage. More for her paramour.

He would not care more for a clean slate than for this child that Sophia carried. He had needed to marry. Had needed to produce an heir, and it seemed that he was halfway there already. Why should he preserve the nation, their sensibilities, and ignore the fact that this was a moment to seize on something that would be an important asset. Truly, he could not have planned this better.

Because there was only one way that he would be able to justify claiming Sophia as his own. Only one way he would be able to justify having her in his bed for life.

The child.

That, no one would be able to argue with. And yes, it would come at the cost of an ugly scandal. The things that would be written about them…

They would not be kind.

Those headlines would exist, and it was something that their child would have to contend with. Something they would have to contend with.

But in the end, the memory would fade, and they would be husband and wife longer than they had ever been stepbrother and stepsister.

In the end, it would work.

Because it had to.

He was not in the mood to allow the world to defy him. He was not in the mood to think in terms of limits.

He had, for far too long.

He was a king, after all.

And for too long he had allowed that to limit him.

No more.

"Do you want to know where we're going?" he asked, leaning back in his seat and eyeing the bar that sat across the cabin.

"I don't wish to know anything," she said, pale of face and tight-lipped with rage.

"Did you love him so much that this is an affront to you?"

"I tried," she said, whipping around to face him, her dark curls following the motion.

"I tried to do the right thing. I tried to do what you asked of me. I was willing to—"

He could not hear her lies. He held up a hand and stopped her speaking. "You were willing to try to pass my child off as another man's. For that, I cannot forgive you."

"You were willing to let me marry another man," she said. "Only when you found out that I was carrying your child did you try and stop it. You took my virginity in a garden. You gave no thought to protecting me. You took advantage of my innocence. You were going to let another man have me. For that, I cannot forgive *you*." She looked away from him again, pressing one hand to her stomach. "He knew it was not his child, Luca. Whatever you think of me, I would not try and convince another man that this baby was his."

"Does he know it's mine?"

She looked toward him, her dark eyes flashing. "I told him it was the one thing we could never speak of."

"I know you only found out yesterday," he said.

"How did *you* find out?" she asked.

"The palace physician reports directly to me, Sophia. In these matters, there is no privacy."

Her face drained of the rest of its color, her entire frame shaking with rage. And perversely, even in the moment, he found his eyes drawn, outlined to perfection by the sweetheart neckline of the gown, to the delicate swell of her breasts.

A sickness. Sophia would always be his sickness.

"How dare you?"

"I dare *everything*," he said, his voice like granite even to his own ears. "I am the King of San Gennaro. You are pregnant with my heir. You would have me leave that to chance?"

"I was trying to prevent a scandal. And I don't want your obligation, Luca."

"You have it," he bit out. "Endlessly, *sorellina*, and there is no way around that."

"Would you have let me marry him?"

His throat tightened, adrenaline working its

way through his veins. He closed his hands into fists and squeezed them. "Of course," he said. "Because when it comes to matters of the flesh, you can hardly allow them to dictate the course of a country."

"Except, apparently, when that flesh takes shape as a child."

"Naturally," he bit out. "I will hardly allow another man to raise my child. I will hardly sacrifice my son's birthright on the altar of my reputation. On this you are correct, Sophia. I was careless with you. And that carelessness should not come back on our child."

"It might not be a son. It might be a daughter. In which case, you might wish you had allowed me to marry someone else."

"Never," he said, his voice rough.

"You don't seem overly happy."

"Happiness is not essential here. What is essential is duty. What is essential is that I do what is right by my child."

"Yes, I suppose it is what your father tried to do for me. Bundle me up and sell me off to the most worthy of men."

"Yes, and sadly you seem to be stuck with me."

She said nothing to that. He imagined she didn't think he meant it. He did.

He had his darkness. He had his trauma,

and he would never have chosen to lock Sophia into a union with him. But the fact remained, it was unavoidable now.

And if that meant he got to sate his desire in her lovely body, then so be it.

"You will be my wife now, Sophia," he said.

"When?" She said it like a challenge. As if she didn't believe him.

"Oh, as soon as we can arrange it. We're going to San Paolo."

Her expression went strangely…soft. Very odd in the context of the moment, when before she'd been looking nearly feral. "Your father's island?"

"It is *my* island now." A soft, firm reminder that his father was gone.

That, though he would have strongly disapproved of this, he was not here to see it. No one was. Not now.

How easy it would be to lay her back on that chair, to push up that wedding dress and lose himself inside her. Talking was a pointless exercise when it was not what he wanted.

Heat lashed through him. He wanted her. Even in this moment, when all should be reduced to the gravity of the situation, he wanted her.

"This will not be easy," she said, her voice shaking.

"Denying me my child would have been simple, Sophia?"

"That isn't what I mean. Don't be dense, Luca. The world will be watching us. Will be watching and judging and we will be bringing a baby into that. It seemed kinder in some ways to try and avoid all of that."

Rage was like a storm inside him. By God, he couldn't cope with not having power. With having his choices taken from him. "You don't have a biological father of your own. The man couldn't be bothered to raise you. How dare you visit the same fate upon your child?"

"Biology doesn't matter," she snapped. "All that matters is that a man is good. Your father was the best father I could have ever asked for. My own father... He didn't want me. He didn't care for me. He didn't matter. Not when I had your father to call my own. He *earned* that place. He wasn't born with some magical right given to him by blood you can't even see. That's how I thought I could do it. Because I know full well that it's not genetics that make a parent."

"And what about me? You think so little of me that you think I am like the man who sired you? That I am like a man who could walk away from his child and never think of her again?"

"I figured what you didn't know couldn't hurt you. Or your goals. Or the country."

"How cavalierly you played with our fates," he bit out.

"How cavalierly you played with my privacy," she shot back.

"You don't deserve privacy," he returned. "You proved that with your betrayal."

Silence descended on the plane. Luca stood up and made his way across the space, heading over to the bar and pouring himself a measure of scotch.

"None for you," he said, his tone unkind. He was well aware of it. He didn't care. She did not deserve his kindness at the moment.

"You hate me," she said softly. "You always have. Or, if you don't hate me, it's a kind of malevolent indifference the likes of which I have never experienced. I would have said it was impossible. To dislike and not care at the same time. But you seem to manage it."

He shook his head, laughter escaping in spite of himself. Then he took a drink of scotch. "Is that what you think?"

"It is what I *know*, Luca."

"You are a fool," he said, knocking back his drink, relishing the burn all the way down to his gut. At least that burn was expected. Acceptable.

Then he stopped over to where she was seated, leaned forward, bracing his hands on the arms of the seat, bracketing her in. His eyes met hers, electricity arcing between them. His skin tingled with her being this near, his entire body on high alert. His heart was pounding heavily, his blood flowing south, preparing his body to enter hers.

He wondered if every time he was near her it would be thus. And concluded just as quickly that as it had been this way for nearly a decade it was likely not to change anytime soon.

"You think I hate you? You think I am indifferent to you? If I behaved that way, Sophia, it was only because I was attempting to protect your innocence. Attempting to protect you from my lust."

"Luca…"

He stood up, running his hands through his hair. "I have always known there was something wrong with me," he said. "That I could not trust my own desires. I proved it to be so the other night. But I quite admirably steered clear of that destruction for a very long time."

"You want me?" she asked, her voice small.

"Did I *want you*? I wanted no one else.

Do you have any idea how many delightfully curvy brunettes I have taken to my bed and attempted not to make them you in my mind as I made love to them?"

Her face was white now, her lips a matching shade. "Am I supposed to be flattered by that? That you used other women and thought of me?"

"No one should be flattered by it," he said darkly. "But I feel strongly that no one should be flattered by my attentions, either."

"Why?"

The question was simple, and he supposed it was the logical one, and yet, it surprised him. He had not expected her to come back at him with the simplest and most reasonable question.

"It is not important."

"I think that it might be," she said.

"Truly it is not. All you need to know is that you will marry me. It is nonnegotiable. You will be my queen, and our child will be the heir. If you feel regret over it, you should've thought of that before you climbed on my lap in the garden."

"If you feel regret then perhaps you should've thought of that before you took me without a condom," she shot back.

Heat, white and sharp, streaked through

him like a lightning bolt, and he had to grit his teeth, plant his feet firmly on the floor and tighten his hands into fists to keep from moving toward her. To keep from claiming her. To keep from doing just what she described now again.

"I have no regrets," he said. "I'm not so certain you'll feel the same in the fullness of time."

Sophia felt drained, utterly bedraggled by the time the plane landed, and she trudged off and onto the blaring heat of the tarmac. Her gown was beginning to feel impossibly heavy, but Luca had not offered her anything to change into.

Had she not just spent an extremely cool three hours on the plane with Luca, alternating between stony silence and recrimination, she would have thought she was in some kind of a dream.

An extremely twisted one.

It was far too hot on San Paolo for layers and layers of lace and chiffon. For the crinoline she had on beneath the gown.

The sky was jewel bright, reflected in the clear waters that stretched out around them, like an impassible moat, cutting them off from the world. The beach was bleached white by the sun, shrubby green grass and broken shells the only intrusion of color along the shoreline. And beyond that was the magnificent palatial estate that Luca's father had built just for their family. She had spent part of her childhood here on this island, and she had always thought it to be like heaven on earth.

Right now she did not feel so enamored with it.

But then, right now she did not feel so enamored with anything.

On the one hand…she had never been so relieved in her life. To have been carried out of that wedding before it had a chance to take place. Because truthfully, she did not want to marry Erik.

But it was difficult to think about marrying Luca. When she knew that he was only doing it for the child. When she knew that he would have let her walk down the aisle toward another man, that he would have done nothing to stop Erik from claiming her. Touching her. Kissing her. Joining his body to hers.

It was almost unimaginably painful. That full realization. That on her own she had not been enough.

It was that feeling of fantasy, of being in another time and space, that carried her through. That allowed her to breathe while they were driven from the landing base to the villa.

It was all white stucco and red clay roofing, brilliant and clean construction amidst the spiky green plants that surrounded the house.

The home itself was three floors, making the most of the fact it was built into the side of the mountain, that it overlooked the sea. She knew there was a large outdoor bathtub that faced out over the water, made of glass, as if to flaunt the exclusivity of the location.

She could not understand this as a child. It made no sense to her why someone would take their clothes off outdoors. Or why one person would get into a bath that size when there was a pool to swim in.

As an adult, she more than understood.

Because she could well imagine the hours she and Luca could spend in there, naked and slick, with nothing but the sea as witness to their time spent there.

She ached for it, shamefully. Even knowing that he did not want her. Not like this. Not forever.

They stepped inside the cool, extensive foyer, and Sophia looked around, nostalgia crashing into the present moment like a tidal wave. It was so strange. She could remember walking into this place as a girl. With her stepfather and her mother holding hands as a couple, with Luca the stormy and electric presence that made her feel strange and out of sorts. One that she wanted to run away from as much as she wanted to linger here.

That, at least, was the same.

She wanted to run from them as much as she wanted to run to heaven. Wanted his hands on her body, and wanted to shout and scream at him about how he was never permitted to touch her again.

He had devastated her.

And the worst part was, even as he had fulfilled the fantasy of rescuing her from the wedding she had not wanted, he had shattered her completely by doing so. Because of the reasons surrounding it.

She supposed it would be a wonderful thing if she could simply be happy to have Luca. If she could simply be grateful that he had come for her, regardless of the circumstances.

But she couldn't be.

Was it so much to ask that something be about her, and not someone else?

The fact of the matter was she hadn't been enough for her biological father. He hadn't wanted her. Not in the least. She loved her stepfather dearly, but she had been more of an impediment to his marrying her mother than she had been an attraction. He had certainly come to love her, and she didn't doubt that. But still…

She was loved circumstantially.

With Luca, she wasn't even loved.

How much more romantic that had seemed when he was out of reach.

"It seems my phone has… I believe they say blown up?" Luca said, the words hard and crisp as he looked down at his mobile phone.

That felt strange. Wrong. Because she had been lost somewhere in the veil of fantasy and memory. And neither of those contained cell phones.

"Why?"

"Really?" he returned.

He had one dark brow raised, his handsome face imbued with a quizzical expression. And then suddenly it hit her. She had been so lost in her present pain that she had forgotten. Had forgotten that of course Luca's phone would be lit up with phone calls and text messages. With emails from members of the press, trying to find out what had happened.

By now, everyone knew that the wedding hadn't happened.

Suddenly, her arms felt empty, and she looked around. Realizing then that she had no purse, that she had not taken her phone. She had nothing. Nothing but this wedding dress for a wedding that hadn't happened.

"Luca," she said. "My mother is going to be frantic."

"Yes," he said, scrolling through his phone. "She is. She is deeply concerned that you've been kidnapped."

"I *have* been," she all but shouted.

"By me," he said simply.

"As if that doesn't make it kidnap?"

"I am the king of the nation," he said. "No one is going to arrest me over it."

"That is an extremely low standard to hold yourself to."

"I find at the moment I don't care overmuch."

"Are you going to tell her?" Sophia asked.

"Well, eventually we're going to tell everyone."

"Let me call my mother," she said.

Luca arched a brow. "I do not want your mother on the next flight here."

"You've kidnapped her daughter, what do you expect?"

"I don't want company."

"Why?"

Suddenly, she found herself being swept up off the ground once again. "You have made a bad habit of this."

"I don't find it a bad habit."

He began marching up the stairs, her wedding gown trailing dramatically behind her as they went.

"What are you doing?"

"Claiming your wedding night."

"There was no wedding. And anyway, it wasn't supposed to be *your* wedding night."

"It is about to be." He growled, and he leaned down, claiming her lips with his own.

The moment his mouth made contact with hers it was like the tide had washed over her. And she and her objections were left clinging to the rocks. With each brush that swept over her, she lost her hold on one of them. Her anger washed away. Her doubt. Her resilience. Her resolve.

Whatever Luca felt for her—and she didn't think it was anything tender at all— he wanted her. There was no denying that. He had said as much on the plane, hadn't he?

She had been so lost in her head over the fact that the baby was what had stopped him from letting the wedding go forward, that she hadn't fully taken that part on board. But it was real. It was true.

This was honest. If nothing else between them was. It was real, if the rest could not be.

This was why they were here. The electric, undeniable chemistry that existed between them, in defiance of absolutely everything that was good and right in the world.

She did not taste love on his tongue as it swept over hers. But she tasted need. And that, perhaps, could be enough.

His hold tight on her, he carried her all the way to the top of the stairs and down the landing toward the master bedroom, a room that they had certainly not stayed in before. Well, perhaps Luca had, but she had not. He all but kicked open the double doors, sweeping them inside and depositing her down at the foot of the bed.

"Where is… Where is everyone?" she asked, feeling like she was in a daze. She had only just realized that there seemed to be no servants present.

"I had everyone vacate. Supplies were left, including clothing for you, so you won't need for much. But we need privacy."

"Why?" Tears stung her eyes, an aching pain tightening her throat. She could not understand why he needed this.

This was all too much. She hadn't appreciated fully the protection that had been built into wanting a man she could never have. For her heart. For her body.

Now he was here. Looming large and powerful, so very beautiful.

It all felt too much. Like she would be consumed. Destroyed. Nothing at all of Sophia remaining.

"Because that bastard was going to put his hands on you tonight," he said, his voice rough. "He was going to touch you. He was going to kiss you. Perhaps you were even fantasizing about it. But I will not have that. I will be the only man to touch you. No other. I will be the only man you want. The only desire in your body will be for me. I will be what you crave. Your body is mine."

"You didn't want me," she said, choked.

"No," he said. "I wanted… I prayed…to not want you. There is nothing that will take it from me. And so there is nothing but this. To take you in any way that I can. To have you. Fate is sealed where we are concerned. There is no reason now not to glory in it."

He reached behind her and grabbed hold of either side of the wedding gown, and he wrenched the corset top open. She gasped as it loosened, felt free as the fine stitching that had been so carefully conformed to her body came loose, and her breasts were left bare to him.

"So beautiful," he said, his dark head swooping down, his tongue like fire over one distended nipple.

How she ached for him. For this. Even as she hurt. Even as her desire threatened to destroy her, she wanted nothing more than to give in to it.

She breathed his name, lacing her fingers through his hair as he sucked her indeed. As he moved his attentions to her other breast, tracing a circle around one tight bud with the tip of his tongue.

"You're right," she said, her voice trembling. "This is madness."

"I knew it would destroy us, Sophia. I knew it could bring down an entire kingdom. But now here we are. There is nothing on earth I have wanted to be rid of more than this desire for you," he said, his voice low, tortured. "And good God I want to burn."

It was like fire. His touch branding her as he removed the layers of clothing from her body. As he left her completely naked except for her high heels, as he pushed her down onto the bed and spread her thighs wide, exposing the most intimate part of her body to his gaze.

He got down on his knees then, grabbing hold of her hips and forcing her toward his mouth.

"Luca," she said, shocked, appalled that he would do such a thing.

"This has been my greatest desire," he said. "Even more than sinking into your tight, wet body, I have wanted to taste you. I have wanted you coating my tongue, my lips. Sophia…"

He dipped his head then, that wicked, electric tongue swirling over the bundle of nerves at the apex of her thighs, tracing a line down to the entrance of her body and drawing the evidence of her desire from her. He added his fingers then, penetrating her, coaxing pleasure from deep inside her. It was too much. It was not enough. It was like a sharp pain that ran deep inside her. That could only be satisfied by him. Only him.

He pressed two fingers into her while he continued to lave her with the flat of his tongue, and she shattered completely. There were no thoughts in her head. Not about a wedding that might have been, not about the man who was supposed to strip this down off her tonight, not about scandal, not about anything. Nothing but this. The extreme heat bursting through her like light in the darkness.

He moved away from her then, his gaze predatory as he unbuttoned the crisp white shirt he wore, as he pushed his jacket from his shoulders and the shirt followed suit.

She could only stare at him. At the beautiful, perfect delineation of his muscles, the dark hair sprinkled there. Could only watch as his clever, masculine fingers made quick work of his belt, of his pants, as he left every last inch of his clothing on the floor, revealing powerful, muscular thighs and the thick, hard part of him that made him a man.

She'd had him inside her once. She would again. Even now, it seemed impossible.

If she had been able to see him the night she had been a virgin she would've been much more apprehensive.

At least now she knew that such fullness in size brought pleasure.

He growled, moving toward her with the liquid grace of a panther. Then he grabbed hold of her hips again, lifting her completely off the bed and throwing her back, coming to settle himself between her legs and thrusting into her with one quick, decisive movement.

Their coupling washed away everything. Like a cleansing fire, destroying the hay and the stubble, all of the temporary things, and leaving behind what was real.

This.

This connection between them that existed for no reason she could see other than to torture them. That remained.

Because whatever it was, it was real.

Each thrust of his powerful body within hers brought her to new heights, and she met each and every movement. With one of her own.

Until he shattered. Until, on a harsh growl, he spent himself deeply within her, and she was powerless to do anything but follow him over that precipice. When it was over, she held him. Because holding on to him was the only way to hold things together.

And she feared very much that the moment she let go, everything was going to fall apart.

Including her.

CHAPTER NINE

HE LEFT HER there in the expansive bed all by herself. Her dress was torn, past the point of fixing, and though he had mentioned there would be a new wardrobe supply for her here, she had no idea where said wardrobe was. Not that she had gone poking around.

She felt too...something. Sad. Bereft, almost, but also boneless and satisfied in a way she never had been before. Or, if she could compare it to anything, it was the way she had felt after their first time. Not happy, no. There was no room between them for something so simple as happy.

It was more like she was lying in the rubble of a building that had needed demolition.

That didn't make it easy. It didn't make it less of a pile of rubble. But there was something inevitable about all of it that made something in this a relief.

Even as it was a sharp pain, like being stabbed in the center of her chest.

She needed to call her mother. She knew full well that Luca did not want her to divulge their location. But he had left her. And there was a phone on the desk. Unless he had done something truly diabolical and cut the line, there was nothing stopping her from getting in touch with the one person who truly needed to know that she was okay.

She wrapped herself several times in the feather-soft white sheet, making sure it was secure at her breasts, before going to the phone and with trembling hands picking up the receiver and listening for the dial tone.

It had one. So, provided she could dial off the island, she should be able to get in touch with her mother.

"Let's see," she mumbled as she typed in the country code for San Gennaro followed by her mother's number.

The phone rang just once before her mother answered. "Hello?"

"Mom," Sophia said.

"Where are you?" her mother asked, panic lacing each word. "Are you safe?"

"Yes," she said.

It was true that she was physically safe. Emotionally was another matter.

"What happened? You were at the chapel and ready, and Luca went in to fetch you and… Is Luca with you?" her mother asked.

"Luca…" The rest of the sentence died.

"What is it?"

"Luca is the reason that I've gone missing," Sophia finished.

The silence on the other end was brittle, like a thin pane of glass that she was certain would splinter into a million pieces and shatter if she breathed too deeply.

"Is he?" her mother asked finally.

"There's something I have to tell you…"

"Oh, Sophia," her mother said, the words mournful. "I had hoped… I had hoped that you had put your feelings for him behind you."

"It's his baby, Mother," she said, the words coming out raw and painful.

More silence. But this one was full. Of emotion. Of words left unspoken. Sophia couldn't breathe.

"I see," the queen finally responded.

"We didn't mean for… I tried… He tried." She closed her eyes, swallowing hard. "We did try."

"Just tell me he never took advantage of

you when you were younger." There was an underlying venom in her words that left Sophia in no doubt her mother would castrate Luca if the answer was yes.

Sophia shook her head, then realized her mother couldn't see. "No. Never. It was just… This time was the first time. The time that we…the pregnancy, I mean. That was the first time"

"I knew," her mother whispered. "But I hoped that it would pass. For both of you."

"You knew that he… That he had feelings for me?"

"I knew that he *desired* you. Far sooner than he should have. And I told his father to keep him away from you. There was no future for the two of you, Sophia. You have to understand that."

"I do," she said. "Why do you think I was prepared to marry another man?"

"Yes, well, that has created quite a scandal."

"Just wait until they find out what actually happened. I imagine my running off before the wedding is not half as salacious as the fact that I have run off with my stepbrother because I'm having his baby."

Her mother groaned, a long, drawn-out sound. "Sophia… The scandal this will cause."

Sophia cringed, feeling desperately sad

to hear such distress in her mother's voice. "I'm so sorry. So very sorry I disappointed you."

Her mother's voice softened. "I'm not disappointed. But it's a hard road, Sophia. Being married to a king. And that's simply when you're a commoner. I cannot imagine how difficult things will be for you and Luca. All things considered. I had hoped that you could avoid it."

"We did. Until we couldn't."

She was embarrassed to be talking with her mother in this frank fashion. Until only recently she had been a virgin, after all, and now she was confessing that she had been overwhelmed by a state of desire. Her mother knew full well what that meant.

"If it was love…" Her mother trailed off.

Sophia's shoulders stiffened, her back going straight, a pain hitting her in the stomach. "If it was love, I never would have pretended I might be able to marry Erik. Luca does not love me."

But she did wonder if perhaps marrying Erik had been about running away. Not from scandal, not even from this conversation with her mother.

From all that Luca made her feel. All he made her want.

"He is a good man," her mother said as if trying to offer her some consolation.

"I know he is. Too good for such a scandal."

"But too good to turn away from his responsibility. Still… I have to wonder if it would've been better if he would have allowed you to marry Erik."

Those words went through her like a lance. "Why?"

"If he can't love you…"

Her mother's choice of words there was interesting. If he couldn't love her. Did that mean that her mother thought she was difficult to love, too? Or did she believe that Luca had a difficult time loving?

In many ways Sophia wondered if they were both true.

She didn't want to love him. That much was certain. Whatever she felt was far too bright and painful all on its own.

"I'm not sure I love him," she said truthfully. "I only know that whatever this is between us is undeniable. And he has chosen to make a scandal. I will only go so far to protect him. I'm not going to force him to disavow his child."

"Of course not. But, Sophia, it's going to

be such a difficult life. Where are you? I feel like I should come and get you."

"I—"

The door opened and she turned sharply. Luca was standing there, regarding her with dark eyes. His expression was like a storm, his mouth set into a firm line.

"I have to go."

She hung up the phone, much to her mother's protests. And then Luca walked over to the phone and unplugged the power cord from the base. "I do not wish to be disturbed," he said. "How much did you tell your mother?"

"I told her that I'm having your baby."

He chuckled, bitter and hard. "I imagine her faith in me is greatly reduced by this news."

Sophia wrapped her arms around herself. "She said that she always knew. That you wanted me. That I wanted you."

"Fascinating," he said, not sounding at all fascinated. "But you had no idea, did you?"

"I didn't," she said truthfully. "I thought you despised me."

"You refused to be any less attractive to me, no matter how the years went on. You refused to shrink. You refused to be invisible. I certainly despised you, Sophia, but my desire for you is not exclusive from that."

"That's beautiful, Luca. Perhaps you should take up poetry."

"How's this for poetry? You're mine now." He took a step toward her, grabbing hold of the sheet that she had resolutely wrapped around her curves, and he pulled her to him, wrenching the soft, exquisite cotton from her body. "There is to be no doubt of that."

She stood there, naked and trembling, feeling hideously exposed in ways that went well beyond her skin.

"Then that makes you mine," she shot back, feeling run out and fragile after the day she had had. "Doesn't it?"

His dark eyes sharpened. "I'm not sure I get your meaning."

"If I belong to you, then I require nothing less. If we are to be married, Luca, I will be the only woman in your bed. You have all of me or you have none of me."

"I was never going to be unfaithful to whatever wife I took. I would hardly be unfaithful to you."

Electricity crackled between them, and neither spoke what was so patently obvious. So obvious that it lit the air between them with electricity.

That at least for now, there was no chance either of them would take another to their beds. They would have to exhaust the intense desire between the two of them first, and at the moment Sophia could not imagine it. Granted, she was new to sex, but she had a feeling that what existed between herself and Luca was uncommon in every way.

"What are you going to do?" she asked, her voice small, taking a step away from him.

"Tonight? Tonight I intend to take you back to my bed, spread you out before me and feast on you until you're crying out my name. Until my name is synonymous with *lover*, not *brother*."

His words set a rash of heat over her body. "I mean, about us. About telling the world about us. About our upcoming marriage. About…what we are going to do next."

"I'm going to make a press release to go out tomorrow morning. And you and I will stay here incommunicado until some of the furor dies down. Then I will marry you. Not in that dress," he said, looking at the scrap of white on the floor.

"I think that dress is beyond saving now," she mused.

He looked at her, his dark eyes suddenly bleak. "Who knew I would have something in common with a gown."

But before she had a chance to question

such an odd statement, she was back in his arms, and he was kissing her again. And she had a feeling that there would be no more talking tonight.

The next morning Luca was full of purpose when he awoke. Sophia was naked, soft and warm, pressed up against his body, one breast resting at his biceps. She was sleeping peacefully, her dark hair a halo of curls on the pillow around her head. He had done it. He had destroyed everything.

It was strangely satisfying. A perfect and sustained string of curses directed to his mother even if it was going to have to make its way into the beyond.

A scandal she would not be able to squash.

He supposed it was unkind to think poorly of one's dead mother. But he could not find a kind thought for his own.

Strange, how he spent very little time thinking about her. He had already made decisions about himself, about his life, based on the events that had occurred in his childhood. He didn't have to think about them every day.

Truthfully, he didn't even have to think about them yearly. He spent a great deal of time not pondering the ways in which he was damaged, and even when he didn't think of it, typically in reference to why he had to keep his hands off Sophia—a horse that had well and truly left the barn now—it was only in terms of his scarred soul, not in terms of actual events.

This forced him to think of it. The fact that his responsible, pristine image was about to be destroyed, made him think of it.

No one can ever know about this. If your father knew about Giovanni our marriage would be over. And can you imagine what people would think of you? They would never forget, Luca. It is all you would ever be.

He gritted his teeth and got out of bed, staring out the window at the ocean below.

He had a press release to prepare.

He set about to doing just that, contacting his palace staff and letting his majordomo know exactly what had transpired. Exactly what would be happening from here on out. If the other man was shocked, he did not let on. But then, he supposed it was in the other man's job description to remain impassive about such things.

Luca also left instruction to keep his and Sophia's location secret.

With that taken care of, Luca decided that he needed to figure out what he was going to do with his fiancée. That was how he would think of her from now on. Until, that was, he was able to think of her as his wife. She was no longer first and foremost his stepsister.

In his mind, she never had been.

And that meant that he had to get to know her.

He had avoided that. For years he had avoided that. Of course he had. He had not wanted to foster any kind of attraction between them.

It had turned out that was futile anyway, because the attraction between them had been hell-bent on growing no matter what either of them did.

Now the fact remained, he was going to marry her, and he didn't know her at all.

That was not actually a point of contention for him, but he would have to be able to make conversation about her. They would have to be able to come to an accord on how they talked about their relationship.

And he had a feeling that Sophia would want to feel as if she knew him.

He had done what he had intended to do by bringing her here to the island. He had isolated her. And he had managed to get her into proximity with him. To keep her from marrying Erik. But he would not be able to keep her here forever. That meant that something other than kidnap was going to have to bind them. Eventually. Something other than sex would help, as well.

Although at the moment the sex was enough for him.

His staff had generously stocked the kitchen with a basket of croissants. Opening the fridge, he found a tray of fruit, figs and dates. Cheeses. Then, there was a pot of local honey in a small jar on the counter. He cobbled those things together, along with herbal tea, and brought them up to the bedroom. When he opened the door, Sophia shifted, making a sleepy sound.

She opened her eyes, and he could see the exact moment her vision came into focus.

She frowned. "Is that for me?"

"Yes," he said, sitting down on the edge of the bed.

He was gratified to see that her gaze drifted away from the food and onto his chest, which was still currently fair. Her cheeks flushed, and she looked away.

It pleased him to see that she was not immune to him.

That someone so soft and lovely could be so affected by him.

He shoved that thought to the side.

"That's...kind of you." She shifted, pushing herself into a sitting position, holding her sheets against her breasts modestly. "What is this?" She opened up the pot sitting on the tray and frowned deeply. "This isn't coffee."

"You're pregnant," he pointed out. "I believe I recall hearing that pregnant women should not drink caffeine."

"Not *too much* caffeine." She sounded truly distressed. "That doesn't mean I have to drink...herbs."

"I was only doing the best I could. I'm not an expert."

"That might be a first," she said.

"What?"

She treated him to a smile that was almost impish. Something he wasn't used to having directed at him. "You admitting that you don't know everything."

"Sophia..." he said, his tone full of warning.

"You can't tell me it isn't true."

"I was raised to be arrogant. It's part and parcel to being in charge."

"Really?" she asked.

"Nobody wants an uncertain king."

"Perhaps. But no one wants an insufferable husband, either."

Neither of them spoke for a moment. Sophia reached into the basket and procured herself a croissant.

"You like coffee," he said.

She lifted a shoulder. It was gloriously bare and he knew now from experience that her skin was as soft as it looked. He wished to lick her. If only because he had spent so many years not licking her. "Yes."

"I didn't know that."

"Almost everyone likes coffee. Or needs it, if it comes down to it."

"But we have never discussed what you like. Or what you don't like."

She looked thoughtful for a moment, and that should've been an indicator that this was not going according to plan, as he really should have guessed that Sophia was never going to be anything like compliant.

"Well," she said, "I like coffee, as established. My hobbies include getting fitted for wedding gowns that will eventually be torn off my body, and being kidnapped and spirited away to a private island."

Luca cast her a hard look. "Much more exotic than stamp collecting, you have to admit."

"Indeed. Although, my wretched dress is not going to increase in value. A stamp collection might."

"I beg to differ. By the time news of our union hits global media I imagine that torn gown will be worth quite a bit."

Sophia frowned, grabbing a strawberry from the fruit tray and biting into it angrily. "Global media," she muttered around the succulent fruit.

"There is no way around it. We are a headline, I think you will find."

"I tried *not* to find."

"Sophia," he said, suddenly weary of games. "There was no other alternative. No other outcome, and you know that. It was always going to be this."

He meant because of the baby. And yet, he couldn't escape feeling that there was something else in those words. Some other, deeper truths being hinted at.

"We tried," she said, sounding desolate.

"Not that night. Not the night of the ball."

She looked up at him, her expression quizzical. "Really?"

"You know it's true," he said. "Had I tried, I would never have touched you. But I didn't. It was simply that what I wanted became so much more powerful than what I should do. And I could not… Could not allow him to touch you."

"We would have allowed him to touch me last night," she said quietly, picking at a fig.

"He didn't," Luca said. "That's all that matters."

"Luca," she said, looking up at him, her expression incisive. "Why is reputation so important to you? I mean, beyond the typical reasons. Beyond the reasons that most rulers have. You have never been… I knew your father. I loved him. As my own father. He was the only father I ever knew. He was serious, and he treated his position with much gravity. But it's not like you. You do everything with such gravity. And I… Truthfully, whether you believe me or not, part of the reason I didn't tell you is that I didn't want to put this on you. I know how much your country means to you…"

"Not more than my child," he said, fire rising up in his chest, bile in his throat. "Nothing matters more than my child, Sophia, you must know that. The moment those test results came across my desk I had to know. I will not sacrifice my child on an altar with my country's name stamped onto it. With my reputation on it. My name is only a name. The baby you carry is my blood." He took a deep breath. "What good is a legacy if you don't defend the ones who are supposed to carry it out when you die?"

"I'm sorry," she said, and she sounded it. "You're right. For all that we…" She squeezed her eyes shut. "For all that I have carried a certain fascination for you for a great number of years, I don't know you." She opened her eyes, tears glistening in them. "If I could guess at this so wrong, then it is apparent there are things I don't know."

"You're not wrong," he said, the word scraping his throat. "On any score with this, I would have protected the name. But not at the expense of a child."

It was the breaking point. Because if the name didn't matter, then what he had endured, then the lack of action his mother had taken to defend him, would be null and void, and that was unfathomable to him in many ways. This was where the corner turned. Where it became far too close to what had been done to him. And that, he could not allow.

"What are we going to do today?" The question was open, honest, and it made him feel strange.

"I had not given it much thought."

That was a lie. What he wanted, what he wanted more than anything, was to strip her completely naked, rip that sheet right off her as he had done last night, and keep her that way for the entire day.

"Your wardrobe should arrive soon," he said instead of that. "And then of course, there is the beach, and the pool."

"Badminton," she pointed out. "We used to play badminton."

"You cannot be serious."

"We're rather cut off here, Luca," she said. "I was thinking of all the things we used to do to entertain ourselves."

He treated her to a scorching look, and he watched as her face turned scarlet all the way up to the roots of her hair.

"We can't do that the entire time," she protested, her hand flinging out wide like an indignant windmill.

He leaned forward, gripping her chin with his thumb and forefinger. "Why not?"

Her eyes widened. "Because... Because... We can't." Her protest was beginning to sound weak.

"I'm going to need a better reason than that, Sophia. As we have spent years not doing it, and I feel that we have much time to make up for."

"Well," she said, sniffing piously. "It's not done."

"I assure you, *cara*, that it is done quite frequently."

"You would *die*." She sounded entirely certain of this assessment.

He couldn't help himself. He laughed. "That's a bit overdramatic, don't you think?"

"No," she protested. "There is nothing dramatic about it. You've been there both times we've, well, you know. I can't breathe for nearly an hour afterward. If we did it all day…"

"It would be different," he said. "But no less impacting."

"Is it always like this, then? Does it just naturally shatter you less and less each time? Is this how it's been with all your lovers?"

He could lie to her. But then, a lie would neither bring him joy nor accomplish anything. Truth was the best option.

"It has never been like this with any of my previous lovers," he said. "I already told you that you have been my obsession for far too long. And there has been nothing that I could do to put a dent in that hunger. And before you… I didn't know such hunger at all."

"Oh," she said, sounding subdued.

"I wished often that it was simple enough to just want another woman," he said. "But it is not."

He shook his head. "There is no way around it. We must go through."

"Perhaps after badminton."

"If you get out a badminton racket, I will break it over my knee." Possibly, he could break it over another part of his body, given how hard he was at the moment.

It didn't take much. He was held in thrall, just for a moment, as the sunlight broke through a crack in the curtains, streamed onto Sophia's lovely upturned face, catching the light behind her wild curls. Sophia was naked in his bed. After so many years of lust.

She was his. There was triumph in that, to be certain.

He was Nero. Fiddling while Rome burned, he supposed. But Rome was going to burn no matter what at this point. He supposed he might as well play away.

"There is one thing I'm curious about."

"Whether or not I take cream in my coffee?"

"No. Why were you a virgin, Sophia?"

She drew back, pressing her hand to the center of her chest, the expression almost comically missish. "Does it matter?"

"The very fact that you would ask that question says to me that it must."

"I never found anyone that I felt… Luca,

if no other man could make me feel what I felt just looking at you, if he kissed me, if he touched me, what was the point of going to bed with him? I would be thinking of you."

He was humbled by that. Shame. A familiar, black fog rolling over his shoulders and down his spine. Yes, shame was his constant companion. And sex was…

It never occurred to him to deprive himself of sex. His introduction to it—such as it was—had not been his choice. And he had set out to make a choice after that, and every time thereafter.

It had become a way of putting distance and bodies between that first encounter.

To prove to himself that in truth, the two experiences were not even the same. But what had been done to him against his will that night was something dark. Something ugly.

Control. A deep contempt for another person's autonomy.

"I was with other people and thought of you," he pointed out. "Unless I made it a point not to. And then, I made sure it was someone who was quite different to you."

"I suppose that's the difference between men and women, then," she said.

"Or simply the difference between you and me," he responded. "Sophia… There are many reasons that I never allowed myself to touch you for all that time."

"Your reputation."

"My reputation, the reputation of San Gennaro, is only a piece of the puzzle."

"Then tell me what the puzzle is, Luca. I feel like I should understand since we are supposed to be married. I feel like I need to understand you."

"We have a history," he said slowly. "One that has been difficult. I cannot… I cannot adequately express to you the way it was when I first noticed you as a woman. The way that it hit me. You were always…reckless and wild in a way that I could not fathom, Sophia, and yet the fact that it bothered me as it did never made any sense. Until you turned seventeen. And suddenly…everything that you were, this vivacious, irrepressible girl, crashed into what you had become. I knew I couldn't have you. I knew that it was impossible. And so, as much as there was never closeness between us, I pushed you away. I don't regret that. It was my attempt at doing what was right. I failed, in the end. And so, those years, that history, is useless to us. Let us forget who we were in the past and why. We have to make a way forward, and I don't think there are answers lurking behind."

She narrowed her eyes, looking at him with total skepticism. He could see that she did not agree with him, not remotely.

But there was no point talking about the shadows in the past. He didn't want her to know him. He didn't want anyone to know him. They could have a life, like this. One where they made love and she teased him. Frankly, it was a better life than he had ever imagined for himself.

He had not ever fathomed that his duty could be quite so pleasurable.

He had resolved himself to a life without the woman that he wanted most. Now he had her. There was no point dragging skeletons out of the closet.

"You have an objection, *cara*?"

"You want to act as though we haven't known each other for most of our lives? You don't want to go back and try to understand who I was?"

"Isn't it most important that we understand who each other is now?"

"Can we do that? Can it be accomplished if we don't actually know what each other was built with?"

"There are no surprises in my story. I was born into royalty." He shrugged his shoulders. "Here I remain."

"You lost your mother when you were sixteen. I suppose that was very painful for you."

"Yes," he responded, the word sharp like a blade.

It was painful. But perhaps not in the way she meant. Not in any way he could put into words.

Losing someone you were meant to love, someone you had grown to hate, was its own particular kind of pain. There had been guilt. Such guilt. As if it were the hatred in his heart that had poisoned her to death. As if he had somehow caused her car to go off the road that day.

He knew better than that now.

But that, too, was a discussion they would not have.

"Today I thought we might have a walk on the beach," he said. "What do you think of that?"

She nodded slowly. "That sounds nice."

Though she still didn't sound convinced.

She would see. It would be better his way.

And if Sophia wanted to share herself with him, he was more than happy to allow it. In fact, he found he was quite hungry for it.

But he would not poison her with the stories of his past.

The poison in his own veins was quite enough. He refused to spread it.

On the score of protecting the family reputation, of protecting her from a life with him, he had failed.

He did not have to fail when it came to everything else.

Sophia was hot and sweaty after spending an afternoon combing through the white sand beaches, finding seashells and taking breaks from the sun to soak her feet in the water.

True to his word, her clothing had eventually arrived, and she had found a lovely white dress that seemed suited to the surroundings. They had walked together, and he hadn't touched her.

It occurred to her that Luca had *never* touched her without sexual intent. Nothing intentional anyway.

There had been no casual handholding. He'd never moved to touch her with affection, only to strip her of her clothes.

Which was why when they had been on their return trip to the estate she had looped her fingers through his and taken control of that situation.

She had almost immediately wished that she hadn't. It had been so impacting. So very strange. To hold Luca's hand. Like they were a couple. Not just secret, torrid lovers, but something much gentler and sweeter, too.

Strange, because there was no real gentleness in their interaction.

Although, it had been quite a nice thing he'd done this morning with the fruit. The herbal tea notwithstanding.

When they returned to the villa, dinner had been laid out for them on the deck that overlooked the sea. A lovely spread of fresh seafood and crisp, bright vegetables.

All a little bit healthy for her taste. Though that concern was answered at the end of the meal when Luca went into the kitchen and returned a moment later with the truly sinful-looking dessert made of layers of cream, meringue and raspberry.

Sophia took a bite of the decadent dessert and closed her eyes, listening to the sound of the ocean below, the sun still creating warmth, even as it sank down into the sea. A breeze blew gently through her hair, lifting the heavy curls off the back of her neck, cooling her.

For a moment she had the horrible feeling that if she opened her eyes she would find that Luca wasn't really there. That she had somehow hallucinated all of this in order to survive the wedding.

That in reality she was on her honeymoon with Erik. Because of course it had to be a fantasy that Luca had come to claim her. That he had whisked her out of that waiting room in the back of the chapel and spirited her off to a private island.

But no. When she opened her eyes there he was. Regarding her closely, his dark, unfathomable eyes assessing her. The remaining light of the sun shone brilliantly on his razor-sharp cheekbones, highlighting the rough, dark whiskers that had grown over his square jaw. She did not think he had shaved since they had arrived.

She suddenly had the urge to watch him shave. To watch him brush his teeth.

To claim all those little intimate moments for herself. Those routine things that were so easy to take for granted. She wanted to be close to him.

That was the sad thing. She had made love to him a few times now, and still, she didn't feel…like they were close.

Physically, they had been as close as two people could be. But there was still a gulf between them. She wanted to know what had created him. This good, hard man who clung to his principles like a mountain climber holding on to the face of a rock.

He fascinated her, this man. Who only ever let his passion unleash itself in the bedroom. Who was otherwise all things reserved and restrained.

That he had been hiding his desire for her for so many years was a revelation.

But he didn't *want* her to know him. He had made that clear.

She understood now why her mother had sounded so upset on the phone. It wasn't simply the issues that they would have with the press. But the pain she would experience, having feelings for her husband that far outweighed the feelings he had for her. Of wanting more of him than he would ever share. Luca desired her. He wanted her body. He'd had it. But sex and intimacy were not the same things.

That fact had become clear when they held hands on the beach and it had rocked her world in a wholly different fashion than being naked with him had.

One thing was clear: sex was certainly the way to reach him.

Because it was the only time when his guard was down. Of course, hers was equally reduced when they were making love. He

did things to her... Made her feel things...
Things she had not imagined were possible.
And she wanted more. She had never thought
of herself as greedy, not really.

How could a woman who had been born
into poverty and become a princess over-
night ever ask for more out of life? And yet...
she wanted more. Being with him, finally
having what she had held herself back from
for all that time, had only made her more
greedy.

There was something about today, about
the beautiful afternoon spent walking on the
beach that ended with holding hands, and this
magical dinner, that made her feel a sense of
urgency. Or maybe it wasn't the dinner, or
the handholding. Maybe it was simply the
fact that they were to be married. And if they
were going to get married then it meant this
was forever. And if this was going to be her
forever...

It had been a certain kind of torture, wanting Luca and not having him. But having
him in some ways, but never in others, was
worse.

Or if not worse, it was simply that it was
closer. She couldn't pretend that there was
nothing between them, not when she was
sharing his bed.

He was beautiful. And physically, he made her feel so very much. It wasn't enough.

And maybe she was so perfectly aware of how not enough it was in part because she knew full well that it could be more.

She had seen that passion. She had felt it. Had been over him, beneath him, as he had cried out her name and lost himself completely in their lovemaking.

She wanted *that* man out of bed, too.

But in order to reach him, she imagined she had to appeal to him first in bed.

Not a hardship as far as she was concerned.

But it would perhaps require her to be a bit more bold than she had been previously.

After all, she had been a virgin until only recently. But the fact remained that what she had told Luca earlier was true. She had been a virgin because of him. Because of the way he had made her feel.

That meant he could have any of her. All of her. Because he was the one her body had been waiting for, so truly, there was no reason for her to be timid. Not where he was concerned.

"Just have some business to attend to," Luca said, rising from his chair. "I will meet you in our room."

The meaning behind his words was clear.

But if Luca thought he was going to be in control of every interaction between them... well, she was about to prove to him otherwise.

CHAPTER TEN

LUCA WAS QUESTIONING the wisdom of checking the way their story was being played out in the headlines before he and Sophia left the island. What was the point? He could have simply left it all a mystery. Could have spent this time focused on her.

But no, the ugly weight of reality had pulled on him, and he had answered. So he had done some cursory searches to see if they had been splashed all over the tabloids yet.

He had underestimated the intensity of the reaction.

The headlines were lurid. Bold. Scandal in the palace. A borderline incestuous love affair between stepsiblings that had been going on for… God knew how long.

A good and handsome groom had been left at the altar, the King of San Gennaro finally snapping and claiming his illicit lover before she could marry someone else.

There were one, maybe two, stories that shed a more romantic light on the situation. Forbidden lovers who had been in crisis. Who had not been able to choose to be together until it had been decided for them by fate. By a pregnancy.

The truth was somewhere in the middle. He and Sophia certainly weren't in love.

He looked out the window, at the clear night sky, the stars punching through the blackness. It reminded him of being with Sophia. Little spots of brightness that managed to bring something into those dark spaces.

There was so much more darkness than light. And it was amazing that the blackness did not consume it.

For a brief moment he felt something like hope. Like perhaps it would be the same with her. That *his* blackness would not cover her light, but that her light would do something to brighten that darkness.

But no.

It could not be. Not really. He was not fool enough to believe it. Hope, in his experience, was a twisted thing.

Was for better men than him.

Suddenly, he was acutely aware of the pitch-dark. Of the way that it stretched out inside him. Yawning endlessly.

He needed to get back to her. Needed to have her hold him in her arms.

A wretched thing. Because he should be the one carrying her.

It was amazing, but somewhere, amidst all the granite inside his chest, there was softness for her. A softness he had never allowed himself to truly focus on before. He had been too obsessed with pushing her away. With keeping his feelings for her limited.

It was over now.

He had her. So he supposed…

The headlines once again crowded his head. It wasn't fair. That Sophia should be subjected to such a thing. Already, there had been many unkind things written about her mother and about her when she was young. And yes, gradually, the tide had turned in their favor. And even then, most had seen it as a fairy tale. He doubted very much that people would ever see this as any kind of fairy tale.

In that world stepsiblings were always wicked. And they certainly didn't get a happy ending.

Least of all with the princess in the story.

No. Theirs was not a fairy tale.

Theirs was something dark and frightening, obsession and lust creating a cautionary tale.

One he certainly wasn't going to heed. It was far too late for that.

He turned and walked out of the office, heading down the long hallway toward the room he was sharing with Sophia.

She might be asleep. She might not have waited up for him.

He pushed the door open without knocking, and did not see her in bed. In fact, he did not see her anywhere.

He frowned. And then he looked up and saw her standing in the doorway of the balcony that contained the large bathtub he had built several fantasies around.

She was wearing nothing more than a white gown, diaphanous and insubstantial. He was certain that—even in the dim light— he could make out the shadow at the apex of her thighs. Of her nipples.

"What are you doing?" he asked.

Her dark brown hair was a riot of curls, those generous curves calling to him.

Every time they'd been together it had been frantic as if they were both afraid one or both of them might come to their senses and put a stop to everything. This was different. There was a look in her eye that spoke of seduction.

Seduction certainly hadn't been involved in any of their previous couplings.

He swore, beginning to undo the buttons on his shirt, until Sophia held up a delicate hand. "Not so fast."

"You will not tease me," he growled, taking a step toward her.

"I don't want to tease you."

"Then why are you stopping me from ravishing you? Because you know all I can think of is ripping that dress off you."

"You keep doing that to me," she scolded.

"Perhaps I think white isn't your color. Or perhaps I think the clothing doesn't suit you. But then, the conclusion could be drawn that I simply don't think clothes in general suit you. I've often wondered why I never cared for the image that the palace stylist had cultivated for you. And obviously the new one has done better. But I think the real reason is quite simple. I like you better naked. And part of me always knew that I would."

She looked down for a beat, those long, dark lashes fanning over her cheekbones. The only sign that she was perhaps not as confident as she appeared.

But then she looked up at him, those brilliant, defiant eyes meeting his. Sophia. Always there to challenge him.

"I'm happy to get naked for you, Luca," she said, the way her lips formed the sounds of his name sending an illicit shiver down to his manhood, making him feel as though she had licked him there.

"But what?"

"I require a forfeit."

"A forfeit?" He paused for a moment, the only sound coming from the distant waves crashing on the rocks below, and the thundering of his heart in his ears. "Well, now, that is very interesting. Do you wish me to get down on my knees and worship at the cleft of your thighs? Because I'm more than happy to spend an evening there."

"No. That would be too easy. For both of us. I will take off this gown in exchange for one thing."

"What is that?"

"You have to tell me one thing you have never told another soul. It might be enough for you to pretend that we only just met, Luca, but it is not enough for me."

His stomach curdled. Going sour at the thought. Because there was only one thing that sprung readily to his mind. There was no other living soul who knew what had happened to him, even though at one time someone certainly had known.

Well, perhaps there was another living soul who knew. Whether or not Giovanni was dead or alive wasn't something Luca was privy to. He didn't want to find out. He hoped the man was dead. If he wasn't, Luca would be far too tempted to see to his demise himself.

Though, considering the scandal that had just erupted, perhaps murder would be surmountable. Or at least not so glaring in the face of all this.

Still. He was not going to tell Sophia.

He gritted his teeth, casting his mind back to something… Anything that he might be able to tell her. So desperate was he to have her naked.

"I was rejected by the first girl I ever cared for," he said. "Though I use the words *cared for* euphemistically here, considering I didn't know her at all."

That wasn't something he often thought about. What had happened the night of the ball. Before he had been violated. When everything had been simple and he had been innocent in many ways.

"What?"

"There was a girl who came to a ball that my father threw. There were dignitaries from all around the world." Which was what had allowed his mother to sneak her lover into the palace.

A man that Luca had met on a few occasions and had gotten a terrible, sick feeling in his stomach whenever he spoke. He had sensed that he knew the relationship between Giovanni and his mother. But then later he wondered if really that disquiet that he felt had to do with the fact that Giovanni was a predator. A predator who had set his sights on Luca.

"There was a girl called Annalise. She was beautiful. Her father was a dignitary in Morocco and they were visiting the palace for our grand party. I was entranced by her. She refused to dance with me. But then we spoke for a while. I led her out to the garden, and I tried to kiss her. She dodged me, and I ended up kissing a rosebush instead."

Sophia laughed, clearly not expecting the story. "You were a prince."

"And she was unimpressed with me."

"How old were you?"

"Sixteen. I believe she was eighteen."

"Oh, no," Sophia said, laughing. "You were punching above your weight."

"I had imagined that being the prince in the palace in which her family was staying might lend me an edge."

Sophia giggled, ducking her head, the expression making her look young. Making him feel young. As if perhaps he were that boy he had been that night. Innocent. Full of possibilities. To love, to be loved.

Living a life that would not ultimately culminate in the moment when his mother proved her lack of care for him.

But perhaps living the life that his head appeared to be at that point in time. Golden. Glittering. One of a privileged, infinitely fortunate prince who had the world at his feet.

Though, in this moment, he would give the world in place of Sophia.

"I like her," Sophia said. "A woman who was not impressed with you just because of your title."

"The same can be said for you, I think," he said, taking a step toward her. She took a step back.

"If anything," Sophia said, "I have always found your status to be a hindrance. Imagine what it would have been like if we would have met under different circumstances."

"You would still be younger than me," he said. "So it would still take time for me to see you differently."

"All right. What if you met me at seventeen, instead of at twelve?"

"Perhaps I would have asked you for your phone number."

She laughed. "That's so startlingly benign. You and I have never been afforded anything quite so dull."

"No, indeed."

"I must warn you," she said. "I don't intend for tonight to be dull, either."

"I believe we have started as we mean to go on."

"I suppose so."

"Your dress," he said. "I have given you my forfeit. You owe me mine."

She said nothing. Instead, she raised her hand, brushing the thin strap of her dress down so that it hung loosely over her shoulder. And then she did the same to the other side. The diaphanous fabric barely clung to her body, held up by those generous breasts of hers. He wanted to wrench it down, expose her body to his hungry gaze.

But this was her game. And he was held captive by it. Desperate to see what her rules might be.

He had grown into a man that most would never dream of defying. That was by design. But Sophia… She dared. And he wanted to see what else she might dare.

"I believe it was for the entire dress," he

pressed. He stood, curling his hands into fists, his heart thundering so hard he thought it might burst through a hole in his chest.

She made him…

She made him wild. And he had not been wild for a very long time.

"I suppose it was," she returned. "Though I see that you are standing there fully clothed. And it doesn't escape my notice that the first time we were together you were also mostly clothed, while I…"

"Your dress was still on. Technically."

"I was exposed."

"All the better to enjoy you, *cara*."

She shivered, and he was gratified by that response. "Well, I want to enjoy you. I want you naked."

She lifted her chin, her expression one of utter defiance. Defiance he wished to answer. Though he had a feeling that his little beauty's boldness might end if he actually complied with her request.

For all that she was playing at being in charge here, for all that she was a responsive and generous lover, she was still inexperienced.

He wondered how long it would take for that to not be the case. How many times. How many kisses. The number of moments he would have to spend in her bed in order to strip that inexperience from her. That innocence. Until she would look at him boldly when he removed his clothes, until she would no longer blush when he whispered erotic things in her ear.

He looked forward to the progression, but he was not in a hurry. For now, he would enjoy this.

More than anything, he looked forward to the fact that there would be a progression, rather than a one-off and a garden alcove, like he had imagined it would be.

He gripped the hem of the black T-shirt he was wearing and dragged it over his head, casting it to the floor, making similar and quick work of the rest of his clothes. Until he stood before her with nothing on.

She did shrink back, only slightly. He had been correct in his theory that she might still find the sight of him without clothes to be a bit confronting.

He spread his arms wide. "And here I am for you, *cara mia*. Where is my reward?"

She turned around quickly, and if it wasn't for the heavy rise and fall of her shoulders, he might have thought it an extension of the game, rather than a moment where nerves had taken over.

But then she lifted her arms, taking a slow, indrawn breath, the fabric of the gown slipping, falling to her waist. Exposing the elegant line of her back, the twin dimples just below the plump curve of her ass. Still covered by that flowing dress.

He gritted his teeth, holding himself back. He wanted nothing more than to move to her. Than to take control. He ached with it.

But he waited. Still, he waited.

She placed her hands at her hips, pushing the fabric down her slender legs, revealing the rest of that tempting skin.

And then, his control was lost.

He walked up behind her quietly, careful not to give her any indication of what he planned to do next.

Slowly, very slowly, he reached out and swept her dark hair to the side, exposing her neck. And he kissed her. His lips pressed firmly against the center of the back of her neck, careful not to touch her anywhere else.

She gasped, a sharp sound of need winding its way through the breath.

He drew back, pressing the back of his knuckles to that spot between her shoulder blades, following the indent of her spine down low. She squirmed, wiggling her hips, and he gripped her left side with his hand, holding her still as he followed his journey down all the way until his fingers pressed between her thighs, finding that place where she was soft and wet just for him.

He moved his hand back upward to cup one rounded cheek, squeezing her hard as he slid the hand that gripped her hip around her stomach, pulling her up against him so that she could feel the evidence of his arousal pressing against her lower back.

"I'm growing impatient of games," he whispered into her ear, capturing her lobe between his teeth and biting her gently.

She arched against him, her lovely ass pressing into him.

She wiggled.

"If you keep doing that, Sophia," he said, "you're going to push me to my limit."

"Perhaps I want to find it."

"I'm not sure you do."

"I don't want your control," she said softly. "I don't want you to be solicitous and careful. I know that you are a man of honor, Luca. But I feel that there is no place for honor between us just now." She arched even farther into him. "Indeed, there's not much room for anything between us. It's just our skin, our bodies, pressed against each other."

He pushed his hand down toward the apex

of her thighs, those downy curls beneath his fingers the filthiest pleasure he'd ever experienced in his life.

He pushed down farther, brushing his fingers over that sensitive bundle of nerves, through her folds, finding the entrance to her body and pressing his fingers inside her. She let her head fall back against his shoulder, relaxing on an indrawn breath.

"Is this what you wanted?" he asked. "You want me uncontained? You want me out of control? As if it has not been so from the moment I first laid my hands on you in that garden?"

"You are far more controlled than I would like," she gasped.

"Control is a good thing," he said. "I think you will find."

He swept his free hand up to cup her breast, teasing her nipple with his thumb. "You will benefit from my control," he rasped, drawing his cheek down the side of her neck, over her shoulder, well aware that his whiskers were scraping delicate skin. She moaned. A clear sign that she quite liked his control in the right venue.

"But I don't have any," she whispered.

"Is that what you think? Sophia, you have had control of me for far too long. My thoughts turn on the sway of your hips, my focus shifting with each breath you take in my presence. How can you not know this?"

"You said I was your sickness," she breathed.

"And indeed it is true." He kissed her shoulder. "There is no cure. I am a terminal case. But I have accepted this."

"I'm not sure how I'm supposed to—" she gasped, her breath hitching as he pressed his fingers deeper inside her "—feel about that."

"Feel this," he said, thrusting his hips against her backside again. "And feel the pleasure that I give you."

She reached up, grabbing hold of the hand that was resting on her breasts, as though she was trying to get him to ease his pleasuring of her. As though it was too much. He collected that wrist, holding it in his hand like an iron manacle, and then he took hold of her other hand, bringing them around behind her and holding them fast, pinning them to her lower back as he continued to toy with her between her legs with his free hand.

She shifted her hips. "You're holding me prisoner now?"

"It seems fair. I've been held captive by you for years now."

"Luca," she breathed his name, total capitulation to what was happening between them. He worked his fingers between her legs faster, stroking her slickness over her clit before bringing his fingers down to the entrance of her body again, delving deep. The waves of her release seemed to come from deep within her, her internal muscles pulsing hard around his fingers as she found her pleasure.

He propelled her out onto the balcony, up to the edge of the bath. He tightened his grip on her stomach, lifting them both down into the water, prepared by her already. And there they were calm out under the stars again, only this time, there were no people. Nobody in a nearby ballroom to come out and discover them. No one at all.

He sat on the edge of the tub, whirling her around to face him, wrapping her legs around his waist, the slick heart of her coming into contact with his arousal.

"Out here," he said, "if you scream no one will hear you. Only the stars."

Those stars. That brightness. Her brightness.

"Then I suggest you do your part to make me scream."

He moved both hands down to cup her butt, freeing her wrists as he did. She moved her hands to his shoulders, gripping him tightly as he moved them both across the tub, the slick glide of the water over their skin adding a sharpness to the sensuality of the moment.

"You want to scream?" He moved them over to the glass edge of the tub that overlooked the sea and turned her, maneuvering her so that she was in front of him, facing the water, the reflection of the silvery moon over the waves.

"Hold on to the edge," he commanded.

She did so without arguing, though there was a hesitancy to her movements that spoke of confusion. She would not be confused for long.

He pressed one hand to her hip, and with the other, guided his erection to the entrance of her body. He pushed into her in one decisive thrust, grabbing both hips and pulling her back against him, the motion creating ripples in the water.

She gasped, leaning forward, her breasts pressed against the glass, her hands curved around the edge like claws. She bowed her head over the tub. He reached forward, grabbing hold of her dark curls and drawing her head back, none too gently, as he found her throat with his lips, kissing her, then scraping it with the edge of his teeth.

He rode her like that, one hand gripping her

hip tightly, his blunt fingers digging into her skin, the other holding her hair as he thrust into her in an endless rhythm that pushed fire down his spine and sent pleasure through him like a river of molten flame.

He felt when her thighs began to quiver, when she got close to release. And he slipped his hand to her furrow again, brushing his fingers over where she was most sensitive, not stopping even as he felt her release break over her. Not stopping until she was screaming herself hoarse into the night, out over that endless ocean, up to the stars.

Into the darkness.

Into his darkness.

And when his own control reached its end he grabbed hold of her with both hands, holding her steady while he poured himself into her. His despair, his need, his release, nothing like a simple achievement of pleasure, but the sharp edge of a knife, cutting into him, making him bleed.

Reducing him. Right there in front of her. And there was nothing that could be done about that. Nothing he could do to fight it.

He reached out, holding on to the edge of the tub, bracing himself for a moment while he caught his breath. She looked over her shoulder, those eyes connecting with his. She looked… She looked as undone as he felt, and he could not ignore the question in them. The need. To be held.

He gathered her up in his arms and carried her across the tub and they stepped out onto the balcony. There was a large, fluffy towel folded up on a shelf adjacent to the tub and he grabbed hold of it, wrapping it around her and holding her against him as he brought her back into the bedroom, depositing her onto the center of the bed.

He didn't bother to dry himself, coming down beside her completely naked as she wrapped the edges of the towel more firmly around her body.

She rolled onto her back, letting out a long, slow sigh. She had the towel pulled over her breasts, but it parted just above her belly button, revealing that delicious triangle at the apex of her thighs. He was not going to disabuse her of her illusion that she might be covered.

"Luca," she whispered. "Why do I get the feeling that it isn't the secret of Annalise that stands between us?"

CHAPTER ELEVEN

"I DON'T FOLLOW YOU."

"That's not your secret. You may not have ever told anyone about it, but I think you never told anyone because it wasn't important. I think there's something important. Something you don't talk about because of the heaviness."

She rolled to her side, looking at him, her dark gaze much more insightful than he would like. He felt... Well, he felt naked. A ridiculous thing, because he had been naked this entire time. But suddenly, he felt as though she had cut into him and peeled his skin from his bones, giving her a deep look into places that he had been so certain were hidden. And yet, she had seen. Easily and with accuracy.

"I'm not talking about this now."

"Then when? It's a wonderful thing, a beautiful thing, to have you out of control when we are together like this. But what about the rest of the time? What about what comes after? When we have to live a life together."

He growled, rolling over, pinning her to the bed, pressing his palms into her shoulders. "The dark things that live in me... It will do you no good to know about them." He felt a sick kind of shame roll over his skin like an oily film, as if he had not just been made clean by the water in the bathtub. As if he had not just been made clean by joining to her.

He realized, with a sharp sort of shock, that there was an element of fear buried in his deep reluctance to never speak of his past. Luca was an attractive man, and he well knew it. Not just physically; the women responded to his looks, to his expertly sculpted body and to his sexual prowess. But also, he was a man with money, a man with a title. It would be disingenuous for him to pretend he presented absolutely no attraction to women.

But he realized that the words his mother had spoken to him after that night had taken root deeper than he had imagined. That it would make people think things about him. That it would repulse and appall Sophia if she knew the truth. If she knew the things that had been done to his body, would she want him at all? Or would she find him damaged in some way?

It was an unacceptable weakness. To worry about these things. To care at all.

And that was the real problem. He wanted to pretend that it didn't matter. That he didn't think about it. That it only shaped him in good ways. In ways that he had chosen. But these feelings, this moment, made it impossible. An illusion he could no longer cling to. If he resented Sophia for anything, it was this, most of all.

"Do you want to know why reputation is so important to me?" The words scraped his throat raw on their exit. He didn't want to speak of this, but the very fact that it had become such a leaden weight inside him that it had become something insurmountable, meant it was time for him to speak of it. Because if there was one thing he couldn't stand more than the memory, it was giving it power.

It was acknowledging all that it meant to him.

He wanted it to be nothing. Which meant speaking of it should be nothing. But the ugly turn of that was if it meant something to Sophia... If he had to see disgust or pity in her eyes...

But suddenly, that luminous gaze of hers

was far too much for him to withstand. And he thought that perhaps, as long as she wanted him in the end, a little bit of distance was not the worst thing.

"My mother had lovers," he said. "I imagine you didn't know that."

Sophia frowned. "I've never heard my mother or your father speak of his first wife."

"Yes. Well. It is not because he was mired in grief. Though I think he felt some measure of it, they were no longer in love by the time she died, if they ever were. I think…" Suddenly, a thought occurred to him that never had before. "I think your mother was his first experience of love. I think perhaps that is why the connection was so powerful there was no care given to propriety. Not when he already knew what could happen when you married someone who was supposed to be suitable."

"You… You knew that she had lovers. But you must have been…a boy."

"I was. Very young. At first, I did not question the presence of men in the palace and my father's absence. We had many people stay there at many different times. But it was clear, after a fashion, that they were…special to my mother. It could not be ignored. Mostly, they ignored me. But there was one… He often tried to speak to me. Attempted to cultivate a relationship with me. I was sixteen."

"That was just before she died," Sophia said softly.

"Yes. Giovanni was the last one. It was as if everything came to a head at that point." He hesitated. "Remember that ball I told you about?"

"The one with Annalise."

"Yes. I think perhaps the reason that my memory of her is so sharp is because… Sometimes my life feels as if it's divided into before and after. I know that many people would think I mean my mother's death. But that is not the case. Before and after the night of that ball. I was a different person then. A boy. Protected from the world. That is the function of palace walls, after all. They keep you insulated. And I was, for certain."

He didn't want Sophia to touch him while he spoke of this. Didn't want there to have been any contact between them. He rolled to the side, putting a solid expanse of bedspread between them. She seemed to understand. Because she didn't move. She stayed rooted to the spot he had pinned her in a moment ago.

"That night, after the ball ended… Giovanni had gotten me a drink. It was slightly unusual as he took pains in public to pretend he didn't know me. Why hint at a relationship with my mother? But still. I took the drink. I felt...very tired. And I remember I left early. I assume he then took advantage of the fact that people were moving around. The fact that people were walking through the halls... It was all normal. And anyone who was in attendance had certainly been vetted and approved by the royal family."

"Luca," she whispered, "what happened?" He could hear both confusion and dawning horror in her voice. And he knew that she had not guessed, but that she felt a strong sense of disquiet. Of fear.

He took a breath, closed his eyes. "He violated me."

The words were metallic on his tongue. There were uglier words for what had happened to him. More apparent. But they were still too difficult to speak, because *victim* lay on the other side of them, and that was something he could not admit. Something he could not speak.

"He..."

He did not allow her to speak. "I think you know the answer."

She said nothing for a moment, silence settling heavy around them as flashes of memory replayed themselves in his mind. Flashes were all he had. A blessing of sorts, he supposed. A strange, surreal state brought about by whatever drug he'd been given.

"Why wasn't he arrested? Why weren't you protected?"

"It never happened again," he said gravely. No. He had gone straight to his mother. Because there had been no one else to speak to about it. How could he tell his father what had happened, at the hands of his mother's lover? To do so would mean to uncover her. But surely, she would protect her son.

She had not.

Not really.

Her version of protection had been to ensure that Giovanni didn't come to the palace anymore. She had cut off her association with him, but she did not, would not, push punishing him. For her own reputation.

"The reputation of the nation," he said, his throat tightening. "It was the most important thing."

"How can you say that? Of course it wasn't. Your safety was the most important thing. Justice for what had been done to you."

Her lip was curled upward, an expression of disgust. Likely directed at what had been done to him, and not at him. But still, somehow it felt all the same.

"What does that mean in context with an entire nation of people?"

"You were raped," she said.

The words hit him like the lash of a whip. "And how is a nation supposed to contend with that? A future king who has been... victimized. Who was held down in his own bedchamber... It could not be. My mother explained why."

"Your mother?"

"There is no point having this discussion. She was correct. It would follow me, Sophia. It would be the story of who I was. Something like that cannot be forgotten. Admitting a weakness on that score..."

"You are not weak," she protested. "There is nothing weak about... You were drugged."

"So easy it would be to destroy the throne then. To attack the kingdom. See how vulnerable I am?"

"No," she protested.

"I don't believe that," he said. "To be clear. I was there, and I'm well aware of what I would have been able to fight and what I could not. But that would be the speculation, Sophia. And there is a reason that this does not get spoken of."

"Luca..."

"I have trusted you with it. You asked for

this. You pushed for it. Don't you dare betray me."

He felt some guilt at saying that. As if she would. Of course she wouldn't. She was looking at him with the truest emotion he had ever seen. His mother certainly hadn't looked at him like that. She had been horrified, too. But not about what had been done to him half as much as what the fallout could be. The fallout for her.

He hated this. He hated thinking of it. It was best left buried deep, with the lesson carried forward. There was no point to this. Because there was nothing that could be done. It was dragging out dead bodies and beating them. And there was simply no reason for that.

You could not spend your life punching at ghosts. That much he knew.

"Am I a strong king, Sophia?"

"Yes," she said softly.

"Would I be so strong in the eyes of the people if they knew?"

"You should be," she said.

"But *would I be*? We cannot deal in what should be. If what should have happened had happened I would not have been violated. But I was. I can only deal in reality as it is. And I cannot take chances. Why do you think I did my very best to stay away from you? I have a reputation. Our country has a reputation. And what exists now? It has been built on the back of my silence. And now I've blown it all to hell."

"Luca, you cannot carry all of that. You're a man. You cannot control what people think of you. You're a good man, that's what matters. Not what people think. But what you do for the country."

"So you say. But our standing in the world would greatly be affected by the way the people perceived me. By the headlines. And when it came to my child… There was no choice. In that I would choose him."

"You should have chosen yourself," she said softly. He bit back the fact that it was his mother who hadn't chosen him. So why the hell should he?

He had already stripped his soul bare, had already confessed to the kind of weakness and shame that made his skin crawl to even consider. The last thing he was going to do was go further into mommy issues.

"I chose San Gennaro," he said instead.

"Luca…"

He got out of bed. "I have some more work to see to."

"It's late."

"Yes," he said. "But it will not wait."

There was no work. But he needed distance. Feeling like he did, he could not allow her to touch him. He needed a chance to get distance from this moment. To forget this conversation had ever happened.

He had expected… He had expected her to pull back, and she wouldn't. Damn her. She surprised him at every turn.

He collected his clothing and pulled it on, walking out of the bedroom, ignoring Sophia's protests. He pushed his hands through his hair and paused for a moment, only just now realizing how quickly his heart was beating. But he had done it. He had spoken the words. Maybe now… Maybe now it wouldn't matter.

He walked down the hall toward his office, and when he entered the room his phone was lighting up, vibrating on his desk.

It was his stepmother. He picked up the phone. "It's late," he said.

"You need to come home," she said.

"I'm busy at the moment."

"Luca," she said, "I would not tell you to come home if it wasn't absolutely necessary. This is all getting out of hand. And you cannot simply leave the country to take care of itself."

"What about Sophia? This is for her benefit, not mine."

"Then leave her there alone. Wherever you've spirited her off to, leave her in peace while you come here to deal with the fallout of your actions."

"I assure you that your daughter has culpability in the situation."

"Oh, I have no doubt, but if your only view is to protect her, then leave her behind and come back and address your people."

"You know I can't do that. If we step out, we must do so together."

"That is likely true. But... Luca, I beg you, don't hurt Sophia. She is not from your world. No matter how long she has lived in it... It is not ingrained in her the way that it is in you. That duty must come first. For her, love will always come first."

Yes, and he knew that. Because for her, what his mother had done was unfathomable. While to him... He might resent it, but... In the end, could he truly be angry about it? What he had said to her was true. He would be defined by that experience if the world knew of it. It was difficult to be angry about the fact that he was not.

"I won't," he said.

"I wish I believed you."

"I will marry her. I will not abandon her."

"That's my concern. But you seem to think that is all that is required of you. There is so much more, Luca."

"What else is there?"

She said nothing for a moment. "Come home."

"I will ready a plane for an early morning departure."

CHAPTER TWELVE

WHEN SOPHIA AWOKE to see Luca standing at the side of the bed, wearing nothing but a pair of dark slacks, his arms crossed over his bare chest, his expression forbidding, she knew something was wrong.

"What?" She scrambled into a sitting position and pulled her sheet up to her chest.

Suddenly, last night came flooding back to her. His confession. What had happened to him at the hands of his mother's lover. He had left after that. And it had hurt that he had pulled away, but she had understood that it had been required.

Still. She wanted to hold him. She wanted to…offer him something.

She knew that he wouldn't let her.

"We need to leave," he said, his voice stern.

He walked over to the closet and took out a crisp white shirt, pulling it over his broad shoulders and beginning to button it slowly.

"Why?" She shook her head, trying to clear the webs of cotton from her brain. "I thought we were going to stay here until everything died down."

"We were. But your mother called. She convinced me otherwise." His jaw firmed, his expression like iron. "It is not going to be easy. But she is correct. I have left the country to burn in my absence, and I cannot do that. She suggested…that I leave you here."

"I don't want to stay here. I want to go with you."

He seemed to relax slightly at that. But only slightly. "I feel it would be best for you to come with me. It would be good for us to present a united front. However…"

"There is no however," she said, pushing herself up so that she was sitting straighter. "You're right. If you return without me the rumors will only get worse. Whatever you say. I need to be there. I need to be there, speaking for myself. There is no other alternative that is acceptable."

"You are very brave, Sophia."

Was she? She had never felt particularly brave. A girl who had tried once to gain the attention of her father, only to fail. Who had then spent a life infatuated with a stepbrother who didn't even like her.

Suddenly, it all became clear, as if the clouds had rolled back, revealing a clear sky and full sun. She had spent those years infatuated with Luca to protect herself. If she had ever fancied herself in love with him, she had been wrong. Because she had not known him.

He had never even been kind to her. Had never demonstrated any softness toward her. Had taken no pains to make her feel welcome in the palace.

He had been the safest.

Until the moment he had touched her in the garden, and it all became painfully real.

But until last night, she had never really known him.

She had been attracted to the untouchable quality he had. To the safety that represented. And more than that, to his strength. The integrity that he exuded.

She had admired that, because she had known men without it. Her own father being one of them.

But that wasn't enough to be love.

Suddenly, as he stood there, putting himself back together, after making himself so vulnerable the night before, putting the king back on over the top of the wounded boy, she fully appreciated what that integrity meant. What that strength cost.

That the granite in his voice, the hardness in his eyes, the straightness in his stance, the way he held his head high, had all come with great difficulty.

Anyone who knew his public story would think he was a man who was exactly as he had been raised to be. A man who had never faced any real adversity, beyond the loss of his mother. And what famous, handsome prince these days had not experienced such a thing?

But they didn't know. Not really.

Until last night she hadn't, either.

Suddenly, it felt as if someone had reached inside her chest and grabbed hold of her heart, squeezing it hard. Feeling overwhelmed her. There was no safety here. There was no careful divide created by his disdain, no distance at all. This wasn't simple attraction, wasn't fascination. It was more. It was deeper.

It was something she had not imagined possible. Something she hadn't wanted.

Love, for her, apart from her family, had always been a simple word.

This was more. It created a seismic shift inside her, incited her to action. To open herself up and expose herself to hurt.

The very last thing that love was was a feeling. It was so many other things first.

She understood that then.

Because until then, she had not loved Luca. But she did now. Deeply.

"I must get myself presentable," she said. And then she rose out of the bed, not covering herself at all, and walked over to the closet, where, at the moment their clothes were mingled. Would it always be like this? With their lives tangled together?

She imagined that Luca fancied a royal marriage to be something based on tradition. That they would carry out their separate lives, in their separate quarters.

But their parents hadn't done that. His father, and her mother, had shared everything. Space. Life. Breath.

That was what she wanted. She didn't want to be the wife of his duty. She wanted to be the wife of his heart.

She turned to face him, whatever words on her lips there had been dying the moment that her gaze connected with his. With the heat there. He was looking at her with a deep, ferocious hunger that made her feel…both happy and sad all at once.

Luca wanted her. There was no denying that.

But whatever else he felt…

He was perfect. A man perfectly formed,

with a wonderfully symmetrical face, classically handsome features that his aristocratic air pushed over into being devastating. His physique was well muscled, his hands large and capable. So wonderful to be held by.

But he was scarred. Inside, he was destroyed.

And no one looking at him would have any clue.

She wondered…

She wondered if there was any way to reach past those scars.

Any way to touch his heart.

She turned away from him again, concentrating on dressing herself. She selected a rather somber black sheath dress, not one that would be approved by the new stylist, but one that would best suit their return back to the country. She had a feeling they would be trying to strike a tone that landed somewhere between defiance and contrition. Not an easy thing to do. But they would have to be resolute in what they had chosen, while being mindful of the position the nation was put in due to the scandal.

He was distant the entire plane ride back to San Gennaro, but she wasn't overly surprised by that. He was trying to rebuild that wall. Brick by brick. Oh, not to keep out that physical lust. Not anymore.

But that new emotional connection that had been forged last night…

He wanted badly to turn away from that. And she didn't know how to press it. She had always imagined she had lived the harder life. She was from poverty, after all. She had a father who didn't want her. She knew what it was to go to bed hungry. She'd been fortunate enough to come into a wonderful life at the palace, but it had been foreign to her. Filled with traditions and silverware that were completely unfamiliar to her.

But now she knew different.

Now she knew that incredible strength could mask unfathomable pain. The walls of a palace could not keep out predators when they had simply been let in.

When the plane descended it felt like a heavyweight was pushing them down toward the ground. Or perhaps that was just the feeling inside her chest. Heaviness.

She wished they could stay on the island. That they could stay in a world where rigorous walks on the beach and lazy lovemaking sessions in a tub were the most pressing things between them.

She had to wonder… If they had not spoken last night…would he be ready to fly back today? Would he be so dead set on their need to return home?

She wondered if he wasn't facing his duty so much as running from her.

No, that wasn't fair.

If there was one thing Luca was not, it was a coward. He would forcefully tell her he didn't want to speak of something, that was certain, but he would not run.

"Prepare yourself," he said, the first words he had spoken to her in hours as the plane door opened.

And indeed, his words were not misplaced. Their car was down there waiting for them, but it was surrounded. Bodyguards were doing their best to keep the horde at bay, but camera flashes were going off, blinding Sophia as they made their way down the stairs and toward the limousine.

Luca wrapped his arm tightly around her and guided her into the car, speaking firmly in Italian before closing the door behind them.

"We will have to speak to them, won't we?" she asked as the car attempted to maneuver its way through the throng.

"Eventually," he said. "But I will do it on my own terms. I am the king of this nation, and I will not be led around by the dictates of the press. Yes, we have answers to give. Yes, we must return and create a solid front for the country. But I will not stand on the tarmac and give an interview like some fame whore reality TV star."

She examined the hard line of his profile, shiver working its way down her spine.

Everything he believed in was crumbling in front of him, and still, he was like granite. Protecting his image had been everything, because if it wasn't…

She felt like she'd been stabbed in the chest as she realized, fully, deeply, the cost of all this to him. How it linked to the pain of his past, and the decisions that had been made then.

It made her want to fix it. To fix him. Because she had been part of this destruction. But she hadn't understood.

"Luca," she said softly.

"We don't need to talk," he said, firm and rigid. "There will be time later."

"Will there?"

"We will have to prepare a statement."

Preparing a statement was not the same as the two of them talking. But she wasn't going to correct him on that score right now.

Later, when she was installed back in her

normal bedroom, alone, she wished she had pressed the issue.

But Luca had been forceful and autocratic like he could be, and he had determined that the two of them should not do anything wildly different from normal until they figured out how they were going to handle the public fallout.

She wished that she was in bed with him.

But then, maybe it was good for her to have some time alone.

She tossed and turned for a few moments, and then got out of bed. She crossed the large room, wearing only her nightgown, and padded out to the balcony. She leaned over the edge, staring out at the familiar grounds below, illuminated by the moonlight. She looked in the direction of the garden. Where all of this had started.

She wouldn't take it back. She simply wouldn't.

Not when being with him had opened the door to learning so much about herself.

To learning about love.

The discovery that she had been protecting herself all those years was a startling one, and yet, not surprising at the same time.

The breeze kicked up, and she could smell the roses coming in on the wind, tangling through her hair. She closed her eyes. And for a moment she thought she might be able to smell Luca's aftershave. His skin. That scent that had become so beloved, and so familiar.

"Here you are."

She whirled around at the sound of his voice, only to see him standing in the doorway of the balcony, looking out.

"Did you think I had jumped?"

"I rather hoped you hadn't."

"I thought we weren't going to talk tonight."

"I couldn't sleep," he said.

He pushed away from the door frame, and came out onto the balcony. He was wearing the same white button-up he'd had on earlier, the top three buttons undone. She could imagine, so easily, what his muscular chest would look like. What it would feel like if she were to push her hand beneath the edge of the shirt and touch him. His hair was disheveled as though he had been running his hands through it. Her eye was drawn to the gold wristwatch he was wearing. She didn't know why. But it was sexy. Maybe it was just because to her, he was sexy.

"I couldn't sleep, either." She frowned. "But I suppose that's self-evident."

"Perhaps."

"It's dark out here," she said, lifting her shoulder.

"What does that mean?"

"We can talk in the dark." She hadn't meant to say that. But she wondered if it was true. If this balcony could act as a confessional, like their bed had done last night.

"We can talk in the light just as well," he said, his tone stiff.

"No," she said, weary. "I'm not sure we can. At least, I think it doesn't make things easier."

"What is it you have to say?"

"I hope that you have some things to say to me. But…"

She wasn't quite in a space where she wanted to confess her undying love. But she did want him to know… She wanted him to know something. "You know," she said slowly. "After our parents were married… I saw my father. He found me. Actually, all of the press made it easy."

Luca frowned. "You were protected by guards."

"Yes. But they were hardly going to stop me from meeting with my father."

"I didn't know about it."

"Well, you wouldn't have. You were away at university by then. We saw each other for a while... Until your father refused to give him a substantial sum of money. I was so angry, Luca. I thought that your father was being cruel. Because after that my father took himself away from me. He didn't want me. He never did. But I couldn't see that. Not then. I was only thirteen, and it felt immeasurably awful to have my father taken from me simply because yours wouldn't give him what he needed."

"What a terrible thing," Luca said, his voice rough. "To be so badly used by a parent."

"But you know about that, don't you? I didn't think you did. I thought... I thought for you things were so easy. I admired you. Even when you weren't nice to me. I admired how certain you were. How steady. You were all of these things that I could never be, wearing this position like a second skin. But now I know. I know what it costs you to stand up tall. And it only makes me admire you all the more."

He ignored her, walking over to the balcony, standing beside her. He gripped the railing, and she followed suit, their hands parallel to each other but not touching. Still, she could feel him. With every breath.

"How did you come to be close with my father? After all that anger you had toward him?" Luca asked. He quite neatly changed the subject.

But she didn't mind talking about this. She wanted to tell him. She wanted to… Well, she wanted to give no less than she took.

Or, what she hoped to take.

"He proved to be the better man," she said.

"How?" He seemed hungry for that answer.

"My father quit seeing me after your father refused to pay him off. Meanwhile, I was a wretch to your father. I was rude. I was insufferable. And he never once threatened to remove himself from my life. No. He only became more determined to forge a relationship with me. He refused to quit on me. Even when I was a monster. He could have… He could have simply let us exist in the same space. There was no reason that he had to try to have a relationship with me. But he did. He proved what manner of man he was through his actions. He showed me what strength was. What loyalty was." She swallowed hard, her throat dry like sandpaper. "He demonstrated love to me. And I had certainly seen it coming from my mother. But not from anyone else. He made me feel like I was worth something."

Yes, the king had pursued her. Her affection. He had made that relationship absolutely safe for her before she had decided to give of herself. But when it came to Luca…it wasn't the same.

When it came to him, she might have to put herself out there first. And she…

That was terrifying. She wasn't sure she could.

It wasn't something she was sure she could do.

If only he would…

She bit her lip. "I was very grateful to have your father. He did a lot to repair the damage that my own father created."

"I can only hope to be half the father he was."

"Well, I hope to be as good of a mother as my own."

It was the first time they had really talked about the baby in those terms. It had all been about blood, and errors and duty. But it had been real. It had not been about being a mother and a father.

"Your mother has always been good to me," he said. "She never had a thing to prove, you know. Not a thing to hide. Not like my own mother did. She is a truly kind woman, who had many things said about her by the media. Cruel, unfair. But she held her head high. You are the same, Sophia. I know you are. You will show our child—son or daughter—how to do the same."

She ducked her head, her heart swelling. "I hope so."

"If it had to be that our child was born in scandal, there is no one I would trust better to teach him to withstand."

Suddenly, Luca released his hold on the railing and turned away from her. She felt the abandonment keenly. As if the air had grown colder. Darker.

"Wait." She held up her hand, even though he couldn't see her. But he stopped, his shoulders held rigid. "I don't… I'm not sorry. So you know. I don't regret this."

Only the slight incline of his head indicated her words had meant something to him. The pause he took.

"Good night, Sophia," he said.

She wanted to say more. The words gathered in her chest, climbed up her throat, tight in a ball like a fist. But she couldn't speak them. So instead, she issued a request. "Stay with me. Tonight."

Then he took her by the hand, and led her to bed. And he did stay, all through the night.

It was surprising how quickly a royal wedding could be put together. Certainly, the wedding that they had assembled for Erik and Sophia had come together quickly enough, but this had been accomplished in lightning speed. They had handled the press a few days earlier, making a joint statement from the grounds of the palace, that had been streamed live over the internet and television. They had spoken about their commitment to San Gennaro, and to each other. And unsurprisingly it had been met with somewhat mixed reviews. But he had expected nothing less.

There was no way they were going to have a universal buy-in from the public. Not given the state of things.

They would have to win them over through the course of time. He had a feeling the baby would help.

Babies often did.

They were to be married in two days' time, and truly, he couldn't ask for things to be going much better than they were. He had Sophia in his bed every night, in spite of his determination that they would not carry on in that regard once they were back at the palace, and everything was going as smoothly as it possibly could. In terms of his lack of control when it came to bedding her...

She was his weakness. That was the simple truth.

He was a man who hadn't afforded himself a weakness as long as he'd been a grown man. Sophia had always challenged him. Had always slipped beneath his resolve and made him question all that he knew about himself.

He didn't like it. But he rather did like sleeping skin to skin with her.

Sacrifices had to be made.

There would be a small gathering tonight, of the guests arriving for the upcoming union. Nothing large, like it would have been with more time. Like it would have been if there wasn't a cloud hanging over the top of them.

It would fade. Surely, it would fade.

And if it didn't? An interesting thought to have. He had been so wedded to his reputation, to guarding what everyone thought, the idea that he had no more control over it was...

He frowned. He wasn't even certain he cared.

Sophia was the mother of his child. She was to be his wife. There was no arguing with that. And as she had said to him just the other night...whatever people thought of him, he could rule. And he could do it well.

The rest didn't matter.

"How are you finding things?" he asked

as Sophia was ushered toward him at the entrance of the dining hall.

She was wearing a dress of such a pale color that the sequins over the top of it looked as though they had been somehow fastened directly to her pale, smooth skin. It glittered with each step she took, and the top came to an artful V at her breasts, showing off those delicate curves in exquisite fashion.

She took hold of his arm, looked up at him. "Entertaining dignitaries' wives is a strange experience."

"But it is your life now," he pointed out.

She wilted somewhat at that.

"I am sorry, *cara mia*," he said, "but it cannot be ignored that being queen does carry its share of burdens. Your mother, I'm certain, knows all about that."

"Yes," she said, though somewhat hesitant.

He wondered what the caveat was, because there was one. He could hear it. Unspoken, deep down her throat. But they were walking into a dining room crowded full of people, half of whom were hoping they would be witnessing some sort of glorious meltdown, he was certain, so he was hardly going to broach the topic now.

He sat at the head of the table, and Sophia

had departed from him and made her way down to the foot.

Tradition, he mused, was such a fascinating thing. Things like this… They formed from somewhere, and that demonstrated that humans could clearly create them out of thin air. On a whim. But there were certain points in history where tradition had simply been followed, and not created. As though someone else had made those rules, and human beings were bound to them. As though they could not be broken.

Tradition. Appearances.

Those things had been paramount to his mother, even while she had lived in exactly the fashion she had wanted. And he… He clung to it because it gave him a sense of purpose. Because it made him feel as if what had happened to him—and the lack of fallout after—had been unavoidable.

It was the reason that he was seated across the room from Sophia now, when he would like her at his side.

All of these fake rules.

He was a damned king, and yet there were all these rules.

The rules that kept him from receiving any sort of justice. The rules that prevented him from acting on his attraction to Sophia in the first place.

And the rules that kept him from sitting beside her now. The rules that had kept them from spending the day together.

A strange thing. All of it.

Those seated around him directly had been artfully chosen people. Selected carefully by members of his cabinet. People who would only speak highly of him, and certainly not call into question his union with his stepsister. He was certain the same could be said for those who had been seated directly around Sophia, and those in the middle could fling poison back and forth across the table to their hearts' content, for he and his bride could not hear it.

When the meal was finished he rose, nodding his head once and signaling Sophia to follow suit.

She looked up at him with slightly cautious eyes, but she followed his lead. She had watched his father and her mother do this many times. She knew that she was simply to follow his lead.

They met at the center of the table and he took her arm again, then they turned toward the doors and made their exit.

The guests would follow shortly, but they

had a moment, a quiet moment there in the antechamber.

"Are you all right?"

"Yes," she said. "I do understand how these things work."

"But it's only just dawning on you that your role in them has changed. Am I correct in assuming that?"

"It's a lot of things. Marrying you. Becoming a mother. The fact that I was going to be queen was low on my list of things to deal with."

"And yet, you will be my queen. Tomorrow."

Her skin looked a bit waxen, pale, her gown and her necklace glittering in the dim light, which was helpful to her, as she herself did not glitter at all at the moment.

"It's too late to go back," he said.

She jerked her focus toward him. "I didn't say that I wanted to."

"You don't seem happy."

"I'm overwhelmed. I have been overwhelmed from the moment that you kissed me in the garden all those weeks ago. I don't know how you can expect me to feel any differently than that."

"Well, I suggest that by the time we are in the chapel tomorrow you find a way to feel slightly less overwhelmed."

She lifted a brow, her expression going totally flat. "As you command, sire."

He had no opportunity to respond to that because their guests began to depart the dining room and fill the antechamber.

"With regrets," Luca said, "I must bid you all good-night. As must my fiancée. With the wedding tomorrow we do not wish to over-extend her."

He wrapped his arm around her waist, breaking with propriety completely by engaging in such an intimate hold in public, and propelled her from the room. She was all but hissing by the time they arrived in her bedroom.

"Luca," she said. "We have guests, and I spent the entire day on my best behavior, not so that you could ruin it now."

"My apologies," he said, his tone hard. "I am ever ruining the reputations of others."

She looked ashamed at that. And he felt guilty. Because he knew that wasn't what she meant.

"Luca, I didn't mean…"

"I'm aware. I apologize for using that against you."

She didn't seem to know what to say to that. "Don't apologize to me," she said finally.

"We're going to have to learn how to make this work."

She looked thoughtful at that.

"We don't have a lot of practice getting along. Not outside of bed anyway," he said.

"That is very true." She clasped her hands and folded them in front of her body. Then she let out a long, slow breath and lifted one leg slightly, towing her high heel off, before working on the other. It reduced her height by three inches, leaving her looking a small, shimmering fairy standing in the bedchamber.

"I know how they made it work," she said slowly. "I know why it was easy for them."

"Why is that?"

"They loved each other. They loved each other so very much, Luca. It wasn't a child, or the need for marriage or money that brought them together. They risked everything to be together. Not because they had to, but because they wanted to."

Her words were soft, and yet they landed in his soul like a blow. "I don't understand what you want me to do with that. I don't understand what you want me to say. You're pregnant. Your mother was not pregnant. I cannot change the circumstances of why we are marrying."

"I know," she said. "But I've found that over the past weeks my reasons for marrying you have changed." She looked up at him, her dark eyes luminous. "Luca, I imagined myself half in love with you for most of my life but it wasn't until after that night in San Paolo that I realized that wasn't true."

His stomach crawled like acid. Of course. She had realized she didn't love him after she found out that he had been such a weak victim of such a disgusting crime. That his body had been used in such a fashion. Of course she was repulsed by him. Who wouldn't be? He was repulsed by himself most of the time. Questioning a great many things about him. Questioning his attraction to Sophia herself. If it was something inside him that had been twisted and broken off beyond repair. Something that had caused him to want a thing that was forbidden to him.

"I am sorry to have destroyed your vision of me."

"No," she said. "That was when my vision of you became whole. Luca, you were a safe thing to love. I couldn't be with you. You were my stepbrother. How could it ever happen? You could never hurt me, not the way my father had done. And all the better, as long as I was obsessed with you, no one else could hurt me, either. You were a wall that I could build around myself. A thing to distract my heart with. The minute that you touched me that wall was destroyed. I didn't know you. How could I love you if I didn't know you? I admired things about you. I admired your strength. I admired what an honest man you were. But I didn't know the cost of those things, Luca, and knowing that… That was when I began to love you for real. I love you, Luca. I didn't want to say it. Because I wanted so badly to protect myself. I have been rejected before. I loved my father, and he only wanted to use what money your father could give him. I could not face being the one who tore themselves open and revealed their whole heart, only to be met with nothing. And I almost did… The other night I almost did. But I was afraid. I'm not going to be afraid anymore. I don't want to be. You deserve more than someone hiding and protecting themselves." She swallowed hard. "I love you."

Everything inside him rebelled at her claim. Utterly. Completely. There was no way it could be true. No way in heaven or hell.

"You don't love me," he said, his voice hard. "You want to make all of this a bit more palatable for you. You want to make it easier. But you don't love me."

"I do."

"Fine. Think what you wish, but that doesn't mean it's going to change anything."

"Why not? Why can't it change anything?"

"Because I don't love anything," he said. "Nothing at all."

"That can't be true, Luca. You loved your father. You care a great deal for my mother…"

"Family. Is different."

"How? Your mother was family…"

"I'm going to marry you, Sophia," he said. "I don't see why we need to get involved in an argument regarding feelings. I have committed to you. Why should you want anything else?"

"Because it's not just something else. It's everything else. Love is vital, Luca, and without it… It's the glue. It's not about lust. It's not blood. It's love."

"There we disagree. Because some days it's the promises that will be all that hold us together. That is how life works. Sometimes it's simply the things you have decided that keep you going. You cannot make decisions in desperation. You must make them with a cool head, and only then can you be certain you will act with a level of integrity."

"Fine. I can accept that you feel that way. In fact, it's one of the things I admire about you. You're a good man. You always have been. There is no doubt about that. But there has to be more. We cannot have one without the other. I don't want commitment without love, Luca. I can't."

"Why not?"

He could not understand why she couldn't let this go. Love was nothing. Love was…

Love failed. It left you bleeding on the ground. He had heard it said many times that love did not seek its own, but that was not his experience.

His mother cared only for herself.

He had been a casualty in her pursuit of pleasure, in her pursuit of protecting her own comfort.

He hadn't mattered.

Why should Sophia feel that he did? And why should she try to demand that he…?

It didn't matter. It didn't matter as long as he promised to stay with her.

"Because don't I deserve to be loved? Don't I deserve to be at the forefront of whatever action is being taken? I have been loved, richly so in my life. But… I've never been chosen. My mother loved me in spite of the fact that having me plunged her into poverty. Your father loved me because he loved my mother. My own father didn't care at all. He wanted money. And you want the baby. Is it so much to ask, Luca, that I be wanted for who I am? That I be loved for who I am?"

"I have told you a great many times that you are a sickness in my blood. If I didn't want you then we wouldn't be here at all. There would be no baby."

"Being your sickness isn't the same as being your love, Luca, and if you can't sort that out, then I'm not sure we have anything left to say to each other."

"So you'll just storm away from me?" he asked, anger rising up unreasonably inside him. "If you can't have exactly what you want the moment you want you're going to leave?" Of course she would. Why would she stay with him? That was the fundamental issue with all of this. She could profess to love him, and she might even believe it. But when it all came down, that would not be so. It couldn't be.

Because he was a man who had been used and discarded. The violation he had experienced at the hands of his mother's paramour not remotely as invasive as the one he had experienced when his mother had chosen to maintain her reputation over protecting him. Seeking justice for him.

And he had no idea how to feel about it. Because she was dead. Because he wasn't entirely certain he wanted his pain splashed all over the headlines, and had they sought legal action against the man who had harmed him, he certainly would have been in the headlines.

He didn't know what he wanted. He didn't know what he was worth.

But he knew he wasn't worth Sophia and all of the feelings she professed to have for him now.

She had tried to explain to him how her feelings for him had shifted, but she didn't truly understand. She couldn't.

"I told my mother what was done to me," he said, his voice low. "I went to her. Trusted her. I had been drugged. I had been violated. Abused. And I told her as much. That she had let that man into the palace, and that he had sought me out and harmed me in such a way. She was upset. And she was fearful. But it was not for me. It was for her own self. She could not have my father finding out she had been conducting affairs. She could not have the public finding out that she had been engaged in such a thing. And if we were to bring him before the law, then of course he would expose my mother for what she was. She couldn't have that. She didn't care for me, Sophia. Not one bit. My own mother."

"She was broken," Sophia said. "As my father is broken. You cannot possibly think that I deserve the way my father treated me, can you?"

"That's different."

"It isn't. You're just too afraid to step out from beneath this."

"Because on the other side is nothing. Nothing but the harsh, unending truth that I was nothing more than an incidental to the person who should have loved me simply because of the connection that we shared."

"Luca," she said. "I love you."

Suddenly, the emotion in his chest was like panic. Because she kept persisting even though he had told her to stop. And the monster inside him was growling louder, and he couldn't drown it out with platitudes. Nothing about promises or duty, or about standing tall in the face of an unfriendly press. About being a king and therefore being above these kinds of emotions, needing to rule with a cool head and a steady heart, rather than one given to things such as this. But he could not speak those words. He could not even feel them.

"You cannot love me," he said. "You cannot love me because I do not love myself." He gritted his teeth, despising the weakness inside him. "The man I could've been was stolen from me. I had to rebuild myself out of something, because God knows nobody was going to do it for me. I was broken open. All that I might have been poured out. And when I put myself together I did not make an effort to replace those things within me that were weak. Those things within me that had… That made me seem as though I might make a good victim."

"No," she said. "That's not fair."

"There is no fair in this. I was chosen for a reason. The boldness that it takes to do to me what that man did. Did you ever think of it that way? I was the future King of San Gennaro, and he felt as though he could take advantage of me, and he knew that he would not be punished. He knew that my mother would protect him. He knew that I would not be able to come forward and speak out against him. My hands would be tied. I refused… I refused to be remade in the same fashion that I had been born. I despise what I was, but I like the man I am now a little more. You cannot…"

He turned away from her, closing his eyes

and gathering his control once again. "You cannot."

"Luca," she said, sounding broken, and he hated that, too. She deserved something else. Something different. A chance to be with a man, to want a man, to care for a man, who was not…broken in this way.

"Do you know," he said. "I have often wondered if there was something inherently sick inside me."

"You keep saying that word."

"I know. Because I wonder if it's why I've wanted you so badly for so long. Because there was something in me…"

"No. Stop trying to push me away."

"I'm not trying to push you away. I'll marry you. But I'm never going to love you in the way that you want me to. I can't. That part of myself is gone. It's dead. I had to cut it out of me so that I can survive all that I went through." He shook his head. "I will not change it for you. I cannot."

To change now would be to open himself back up to the kind of pain that he wanted gone from him forever, and he wouldn't do it.

"But you are pushing me away," she said.

"Sophia…"

She took a step away from him. "I'm sorry, Luca. I love you. And I'm not going to marry you simply because of duty. I would marry you because I loved you but I want you to marry me for the same reason. It would be so easy…" Her words came out choked, her brown eyes filling with tears. "It would be so easy to simply let this be. To take what you're offering, and be content with that. But I… I cannot. Luca, I can't. Because I think we could both have more. It doesn't have to be a sickness. It can be the cure. But only if you let it. And if I stay, and I allow you to have me without risking anything…"

His stomach tightened, turned over, and he ceased hearing her. Stopped listening. "If you don't want a man who's been raped, *cara mia*, all you have to do is say so."

"*Don't*. Don't make it about me being scared. I am scared, but I'm doing the brave thing. The hard thing. I refuse to let us live our lives as broken pieces when we can be whole together."

"What are you saying?"

"That for the second time, Princess Sophia is not going to show up to her wedding."

And with that, Sophia turned and walked out of the room, not bothering to gather her shoes. And he simply stood there, looking at them. Thinking this was the strangest interpretation of a Cinderella story he had ever heard of.

But after that came a strange pain in his chest like he couldn't remember feeling before. And he didn't even try to stop it from dropping him to his knees.

CHAPTER THIRTEEN

SOPHIA RAN UNTIL her mind was blank. Until there was nothing but her bare feet pounding down on the damp grass, the blades sticking between her toes, mud giving way and creating a slick foothold as she prayed her legs wouldn't fail her. Prayed they would carry her far away from Luca. From heartbreak.

She was still on the palace grounds, for they extended vastly, and she knew that she was going to have to stop running and get in a car. Get on a plane, to truly escape Luca. But for now she couldn't stop. For now she could do nothing but run.

She stopped when she came to the edge of the woods, and then she took a cautious step forward, the texture of the grounds changing to loose dirt and pine needles, the heavy tree cover protecting her from the pale moonlight. It was cool, almost frigid, there beneath the dark trees.

She shivered. She wrapped her arms around herself, trying to catch her breath. She took another step forward, and another, her dress shimmering in front of her, catching stolen beams of moonlight, flashing in the darkness.

She didn't know what she had just done. Didn't know what her plan was.

To walk into the forest and die?

No.

That was hardly the solution to dealing with a man not returning your affection.

She had been right, in what she had said to him. She couldn't go through with a marriage to a man who didn't love her. Not just for her own sake, but for his.

She had the feeling that many people— herself included until recently—thought love to be a beautiful, quiet thing. A force that allowed you to be yourself. And while that was true…it didn't mean the self that you projected to the world.

Real love, she fully understood now, challenged that identity. It forced you to reach down deep to your essence, and ask yourself who you were *there*. Real love was not about being comfortable. Not about being protected. Real love was about being stripped bare. Was about revealing yourself, unprotected to the other person, trusting that they would not use your tender and vulnerable places against you. That they would protect them for you, so that you didn't have to.

Real love was the difference between hiding in a darkened forest, or standing in the light.

Right now she was hiding in a forest.

She closed her eyes, a tear tracking down her face.

And it was then she realized where her feet were carrying her. She pressed on through the forest. Through and through. Until she found the paved drive that wound through the trees.

Her mother had moved into the dower house some time ago. It was an outmoded sort of thing, surely, as the palace was so large, but her mother seemed to like it. Liked having her own house rather than standing on ceremony in the massive palace.

It gave her a sense of peace. Gave her a small slice of her simple life back. Although the cottage, with its impeccably tended garden, bright pink roses climbing up the sides of the walls and exquisite furnishings was far grander than anything possessed by Sophia or her mother in their former lives.

It was dark now, the white stucco of the cottage shining a pale beacon through the dimness, the roses fluttering slightly against the wall as the breeze kicked up.

The gravel in the driveway cut into her feet, but she didn't care.

She walked up to the door and knocked.

It opened slowly, and then more quickly when her mother realized it was her.

"Sophia," she said. "What are you doing here?"

"I…" She swallowed hard. "I didn't know where else to go. I didn't even know I was coming here until… Until I realized where I was."

"What happened?"

"Luca and I fought. I… I called off the wedding."

"Come inside," her mother said, ushering her in.

There, Sophia found herself quickly wrapped in a blanket and settled on the couch, and before she knew it, a cup of tea was being firmly placed into her hand.

"Tell me."

"He doesn't wish to love me," Sophia said. "Which I feel is very different to not loving me at all. He doesn't want love. It… It frightens him." She would not reveal Luca's secrets to her mother. Because though she trusted her mother to keep confidences, they were Luca's secrets to tell. "He is very wounded by some things in his past, and he doesn't want…"

"He doesn't want to be healed?"

"Yes. Was his father like that?"

"No." Her mother shook her head. "I was. Your father hurt me deeply. Years of being shunned for being a single mother. The casual judgment I faced every day leaving the house. Collecting assistance so that I could feed you. It all left me scarred and hardened. And then I met Magnus. He charmed me. And yes, when we met, seduced me. I'm not going to dance around that, Sophia, since I know you know full well about those things."

Sophia felt her face heat. "Indeed."

"It was easy for him to tempt me into his bed, but into his life was another thing entirely. And I did my best. To work my job, to keep my liaisons with a king private. To continue to be a good mother to you. I thought I could keep all those things separate. That all of those parts of myself didn't have to be contained in one woman. That I could put walls up." She smiled softly. "But I couldn't. Not in the end. But I was hanging on very tightly to my pain. And I realized I was going to have to open my hands up and drop that pain if I was going to grab hold of what he was offering me. But when your pain has been fuel for so long, it is a difficult thing to do."

"I think that's how it is for him. I think his pain has kept him going, because without it…"

"Without it there's only despair. Anger is much easier. Do you know what else anger is preferable to?"

"What?"

"Hope. Learning to hope again is a terrifying thing. And when you have been harmed, you don't want it. You resist it. Those little bits of light creeping back into the darkness are the most terrifying thing. You cannot hide in the light, Sophia. Darkness is a wonderful concealment. But it conceals everything. The beauty of the world. All that we can have around us. But it reveals us, too. The light. I suspect that is what Luca is resisting."

"What should I do? Should I go back to him? Love him even though he doesn't love me?"

"I can't tell you what to do. I don't want you trapped in a loveless marriage. But…"

"If I love him it isn't loveless," she said softly.

"No. It isn't." Her mother sat down on the couch next to her, clasping her hands in her lap. "The king loved me all the while when I could not love him. But he also didn't compromise. He did not want a mistress. He wanted a wife. And as far as he was concerned, if I didn't love him, even if we took vows, I might as well be a mistress."

"So he gave you an ultimatum."

"No. He just made it known he could not fully bring me into his life without love."

"Well. Luca and I can't exactly have that sort of arrangement. We are going to have a child together. And I live in the palace half the time."

Her mother laughed softly. "I'm not telling you what to do, Sophia. I feel there is the potential for heartbreak at every turn with this situation."

"That's not very encouraging."

"It isn't supposed to be encouraging. It's just the truth. I guess the question is… If he's going to break your heart either way… Would you rather be with him or be without him?"

"I don't know."

Except she did know. She wanted him. She wanted to be in his life, in his bed, but it felt like a potentially dangerous thing to do. The wrong thing. Like it would damage…

Her pride. Her defenses.

Perhaps she was more like her mother than she imagined.

Claims of love were bold, but quite empty when the action was withheld until the other person performed to your specifications.

His mother had given up on him. Had put herself before him.

Sophia realized she could not do the same.

Luca was not a man given to drink. He was not a man who indulged in anything, particularly. But he was drunk now. There was nothing else that was going to calm the pounding ache in his head. In his chest. He had sat there, for hours, on the floor of Sophia's bedroom, pain biting into him like rabid wolves. And then he had gotten up and gone back to his own quarters, and proceeded to drink the contents of his personal bar.

Now the pain was just swimming back and forth inside him, hazy and dull and no less present.

And he had even less control of his thoughts now. Chasing through his mind like rabid foxes after their own tails.

He was worthless. Worthless. A king of an entire country, worth absolutely nothing.

He did not allow himself those thoughts. He never did. But in this moment, he not only allowed them, he fed them. Like they were his pets. He allowed them to rain down on him, a black misery that coated him completely.

He embraced, wholly, his misery. His self-pity.

Sophia had spoken of how he stood tall in spite of everything. But here he was, on the floor. Prostrate to the sins that had been committed against him, and to what remained of his own soul. Black and bruised like the rest of him.

Dark.

He was a night without stars.

Sophia was the stars.

He rolled onto his back, the earth spinning on its axis.

He was worthless because he had been treated like an object. Worthless because his own mother had not cared to seek justice for him.

And yet, in the midst of those thoughts, in the midst of that darkness, there came a glimmer.

Sophia did not see him as worthless. Sophia thought he was strong.

Sophia thought he was worthy of love.

And in an instant, as though the sun had broken through storm clouds, he felt bathed in light.

Why should his mother, Giovanni, be the ones who formed his life? Why should they decide what he was?

Perhaps, in withholding what had happened to him from the media, his mother had protected him from having the public form an opinion on who he was, but within that, he had allowed her to form his opinion of his life. Of what he could be. Of what he could have.

He had escaped the press defining him by that night, but he defined himself by it. By his mother's response.

Had trained himself to believe that if he did not act above reproach in every way at all times, that he would be as useless as he had long feared.

Sophia saw more than that. Sophia saw through to the man he might have been. She made him think that perhaps he could be that man again.

And he had sent her away, because he didn't feel worthy of that.

But she thought he was. She mattered more. She mattered more than Giovanni. She mattered more than his mother.

She mattered more than all the stars in the sky.

If Sophia could love him…

Pain burst through him, as brilliant and blinding as the light from only a moment before.

He loved her. He loved her. And he had hurt her. He had sent her away to protect himself. Which was truly no different than what his mother had done, in many ways.

Putting himself before her.

He would not.

He didn't want to marry Sophia because of the baby. He didn't want her because he was sick.

He wanted her because she was her.

Undeniably, beautifully her.

When he closed his eyes, it was her face he saw.

And then, he knew nothing else.

CHAPTER FOURTEEN

THE DAY OF the wedding, Sophia stayed in her mother's house until clothing could be sent. Then she was bundled up and whisked off to the palace, where she checked to see if anything had been canceled.

It had not been.

Perhaps it was Luca's ferocious pride not able to come to grips with the fact that she was going to defy him.

Perhaps he had a plan to try and win her back.

Or perhaps, he had simply known that in the end she wouldn't leave him to be humiliated.

Whatever the reasoning, she would find out later. With the help of her stylist, she got dressed in her wedding gown far earlier than was necessary. And then she began to make inquiries of the staff.

"Where is he?" she asked.

"The king?"

"Yes."

"In his rooms. But you know it is bad luck for the groom…"

"I already had the bad luck to fall in love with my stepbrother. I think I have reached my limit." She picked up the front of her dress and dashed across the palace, making her way to Luca's chamber.

But he wasn't there. Dejected, she began to make the journey back to her own. The halls were remarkably empty, the staff all seeing to preparations for the wedding that might not happen, it seemed to Sophia.

So she was surprised when she heard another set of footsteps in the corridor.

She looked up and saw Luca standing there. He was wearing black slacks and a white shirt that was unbuttoned at the throat. For one blinding second she could hardly fight the impulse to fling herself across the empty space between them and kiss him there. Right at his neck, right where his heart beat, strong and steady.

But she remained rooted to where she was, her breathing shallow.

"Luca," she said.

"I was searching for you," he said.

"Here I am."

He frowned. "You're wearing a wedding gown."

She swished her hips back and forth, the dress swirling around her legs. "Yes."

"You said you wouldn't marry me."

"I changed my mind."

"Well. I have decided that I changed my mind, as well."

"What?"

"I do not wish to marry you simply because you're having a baby, Sophia. You're right. That would be a terrible thing. A terrible mistake."

Sophia felt crushed. As if he had brought those strong hands down over her heart and ground it into powder.

"You don't want to marry me?" she asked.

"I do want to marry you," he said. "But I'm happy to not marry you. We can live in sin. We can have a bastard. We could create scandal the world over and forget everyone else."

Sophia was stunned. She blinked. "No. Luca, your reputation… The reputation of San Gennaro…"

"It doesn't matter. If I must court scandal to prove my feelings for you, then I will do so. It is nothing in the face of my feelings for you. My love for you. And if I have to burn all of it to the ground to prove to you that what I feel is real, believe me, Sophia. My reputation is nothing, my throne is nothing, if I don't have you. I would give all of it up. For you. That was the real sickness in my blood, my darling girl. That I wanted so badly to hold on to this thing that I believed was more important than anything. Was the only thing that gave me value. While I fought with what I really wanted on the inside. You. It was always you. But I knew that I was going to have to give up that facade of perfection that felt as if it defined my very existence if I was going to have you. Please believe me, *cara mia*, I would gladly leave it all behind for you. For this. For us."

Then Sophia did cross the space between them. She did fling her arms around his neck. And she kissed him there, where his pulse was throbbing at the base of his throat. "Luca," she whispered. "Luca, I believe you. And I want to be married to you. Because I want it to be real. I want it to be forever. We could make vows in a forest, and I know it would be just as real, but we might as well give our child legitimacy, don't you think?"

"I mean, I suppose it would make things easier. With succession and everything."

"You're a king. We could bend the rules.

But I feel like perhaps we should just get married."

"I kept thinking there were more rules for me because I was a king. But all those chains were inside me. And all the darkness… It's because I refused to let the light in. I stood there, on the island, and looked up at the stars. And I marveled at them. And wished very much that I could… That I could be more than darkness. That you could be my light. The only one stopping that was me. All along. The only thing stopping it was…"

"Fear. I understand that… That hope is the most frightening thing there is."

"It is," Luca agreed. "Truly terrifying to want for more when you simply accepted all the things you would never have. When you've told yourself you don't need it."

"Luca," she said softly. "You're not broken. You are not damaged. The people who hurt you… They are the ones who are broken."

"I was broken," he whispered. He grabbed hold of her hands and lifted them, kissing her fingertips. "I was broken for a time. But not now. You put me back together."

"We put each other back together."

"I love you," he said.

"I love you, too."

"I did not think I would get my happy ending."

"You didn't?"

He shook his head. "Stepsiblings of any stripe are always evil."

"Well, then I could just as easily have been evil, too."

"Of course not," he said. "You're the princess."

"And you happen to be my Prince Charming, Luca. Stepbrother or not."

"Am I very charming?" He grinned at her, and the expression on his face made her light up inside.

"Not always," she said, smiling slightly. "But you're mine. And that's all that matters."

"That makes you mine, too."

"I choose you. I choose you over everything," she said. She pressed a kiss to his lips, and he held her for a moment.

"I choose you, too," he said. "Over everything."

And though they spoke their vows later that day, it was those vows that she knew would carry them through for the rest of their lives.

EPILOGUE

SHE WAS ABOVE him in absolutely every way. A radiant angel of light, his wife. And never had he been more certain of that than when he looked at her, holding their daughter in her arms.

He had been right about one thing, the scandal of their union had settled quickly enough once the excitement over the royal baby had overshadowed it all. A new little princess was much more interesting to the world over than how Sophia and Luca had gotten their start.

Luca knelt down by his wife's hospital bed, gazing in awe at the two most important women in his life.

"What do you think, Your Majesty?" she asked.

"I think…" He swallowed hard. "I think that with two such brilliant lights in my life I will never have to be lost in darkness again."

* * * * *